Saving Oakley

Safe and Secure

Book 7

Alyssa Bailey

I0667905

Print ISBN: 979-8-9871524-6-1

Saving Oakley Description

FINDING FOREVER TAKES work and involves risks. Big risks.

Psychiatrist Oakley Addison is lonely. She's ready to enjoy a romantic relationship, but not sure she's ready for the work involved. Determined to start looking for Mr. Right, she heads to a conference, a place she hopes to find like-minded people and maybe find a connection. Before the first session, she fights off a mugger, settles a mistaken identity problem and meets the man of her dreams. This week might be more trouble than it's worth, except for the fascinating, enticing man that has swept her off her feet. Putting on the brakes is harder than she ever expected.

Attorney Ryker Bennett is looking for what his friends have, love. The woman he has recently been pursuing is not the "One" and so the hunt continues. Arriving to present at a conference, he finds himself saving a lovely damsel in distress before entering the hotel. His heart says this could be the one, but his logical mind questions his quick decision.

Ryker and Oakley connect, and things heat up before the conference ends and continue once they are home. Just as they commit to a life together, Oakley disappears. Frantic, Ryker turns to his best friend Jac and his operatives to help him find and save Oakley before it's too late.

More in this *Safe and Secure* Series:
Saving Sharlee
Saving Jessie
Saving Ivy
Saving Mallory
Saving Callie
Saving Becky
Saving Oakley
Saving Finley (Fall 2023)

Prologue

Ryker released an enormous sigh of relief as he climbed into his Lexus Sport, ready to head to Dallas for the Military Law Conference. A week of talking about one of his passions with professionals who lived it daily made him eager to arrive. The freedom of being off the clock and taking his suit jacket off was all that got him through the last couple of days. It was also a way to escape the situation he had been nurturing with Finley, his best friend Jac's Marine baby nanny. He'd been attracted to Finley and, along with one of Jac's agents, had been throwing his hat in the ring to win Finley's heart, or at least in exclusive favor.

The last couple of weeks had been grueling, with many of his ongoing court cases appearing before the judge for some sort of action, but he was familiar with that kind of feast-or-famine existence. The tricky thing about this past week realized that all things considered, he and Finley weren't a good match. They liked different things, and she was adamant she was not interested in having children, but Ryker was ready for them.

He wanted to move out of his condo and buy a house with the proverbial white picket fence. Only his place was more likely to be iron gated and wired for sound, but he could paint the iron white. His 2.3 kids could be four, and he'd be happy. Recently, he had said as much to Finley, who didn't seem broken

4

up about the fact that one of her would-be suitors was falling out of the race. If she were honest, she wasn't looking toward parenting or a white picket fence. It was an amicable parting.

He didn't have much time to look for women that might be his match, but conferences were good places to get out there and find someone who wanted what he wanted. With that in mind, he headed for Dallas. It was early Saturday morning, and he'd pulled onto the highway; only thirteen hours to go. His plan was to pull into the parking lot in Dallas tonight at dinner time, check-in, have dinner, sleep twelve hours, then enjoy a leisurely Sunday reconnecting with friends. Monday was day one of the four-and-a-half-day conference, ending on Friday morning.

DOG-TIRED AND CONTEMPLATING skipping dinner for a bed and sleep, Ryker parked his car. He closed the roof he had opened once arriving in Dallas because the traffic had slowed down. Still lots of it, but slower. Not rush hour or holiday busy. Getting out and stretching his legs, he wondered if it wasn't time to look for a roomier vehicle, something more practical. He'd keep this one for fun drives, but for extended drives and daily work. He might look at something he didn't feel poured into at the end of a long day.

His legs and torso were long, but more than that, he worked out for stress relief, and he'd needed plenty of that lately. Reaching into the trunk to grab his suitcase, he heard what sounded like a scuffle in the parking garage. Sounds were louder and carried well in the covered area, so he listened, and when he didn't hear anything else, he closed the trunk. Another sound, only this one was a scream.

He threw his bag under the car, not taking the precious time to return it to the trunk, pocketed his keys, and patted his phone in his pocket to locate it, just in case. As he raced for the sound, he looked around and saw clothes flying in the air. Then an open suitcase was swung, connecting with the man in front of a scared and pissed-off woman.

Racing, Ryker dove for the man and connected; the momentum and size of his body threw the attacker to the ground. He pulled out his camera, took a picture, and asked for a hair tie, which the woman produced with shaking hands. He twisted the man's wrists in the figure eight of the hair tie. Ryker straightened.

"Th-thank you. I've called the police," said the woman. Ryker reached around her, trying to pick up her clothes off the ground. She joined him.

"Do you know this man? Ms.?"

She reached out her hand. "Oakley Addison, and no. I don't even live here. I've just arrived for the conference that starts on Monday."

"Military Justice?"

"Yes," she said as she nodded her head. "Mr.?"

"Sorry, Bennett. Ryker Bennett. What did he want?"

"He never said. Just grabbed me, then yanked the bag from my hand and started throwing clothes around, saying something about consequences and ruining people's lives."

"And you're sure you don't know him?"

"Positive. Maybe he has a mental health problem." She looked at the very subdued man still on his belly. "He's suspiciously calm for a man waiting on the police."

"It does seem odd. Are you sure you're all right? I would have expected you to be more upset."

"I imagine it hasn't set in yet. I will probably process this when it's all over with when I'm in my room tonight." She paused. "Nice cuffs, by the way."

Ryker grinned and shrugged. "I have some DIY friends." He took a surreptitious glance at the woman before him and was impressed. Too impressed. He was attracted, and not in the needy, anyone-will-do kind of way, but she appealed to him. The way she stood, the fearful irritation she exhibited. And she had won the lottery in the gene pool. His cock, which had been on vacation for a while, reacted to Oakley Addison as though she were the answer to his prayers.

Soon, a Dallas police car pulled up, and two officers stepped out. The attacker was immediately placed in the cop's car, and after giving statements, the two officers left with their charge. Quicker than he expected, but Ryker was glad it was.

"Well, thank you for being a good Samaritan. I don't know what the man wanted, but I'm glad it's over. Can I pay for your dinner tonight?"

"Dinner is unnecessary. I'm glad I was close by. However, I would enjoy your company at dinner."

"I would be very lousy company tonight. But I can send a message to cover your dinner for you."

"Don't. No thanks are necessary. I'm heading to bed because it has been a long day. I started early this morning, and after your little adventure, I'm pretty tired. I'll walk you to the lobby if you let me stop at my car and pick up my suitcase."

When they approached his car, Oakley laughed. "Your case is under your car?"

He shrugged. "I had to ditch it quickly, so I tossed it under the car."

"But someone could have taken it."

"True, but I thought a lady in distress was more important than some clothes."

"And the lady in question is thankful."

Parting at the front desk, Ryker spoke. "Don't forget to ask the front desk to ring my room if you need anything." His voice took on that deeper rumble when he wanted his words to be heeded. He enjoyed a taste of dominance and submission in the bedroom when he could find a willing partner. It tended to spill over into his everyday life, but if he had a woman who enjoyed that play behind closed doors, then she wouldn't mind a little daytime tease. It had been a while since he'd indulged, but the natural instincts were still honed sharp.

"I don't want to bother you, but if I need to, I'll remember to do that."

"I'll expect it."

Oakley paused at his response. Would he also take exception if she didn't? Likely. And why did that give her a little thrill? "Thanks again for coming to my rescue. I'm grateful you came along. Have a nice night and a good conference." Oakley walked to the elevator.

"Good night Oakley."

Ryker didn't feel good about leaving Oakley alone. He'd overheard the officer ask her name. Oakley Addison. It verified what she'd told him. Being an attorney for some fairly high-profile cases over the years, he learned to check the validity of all important information. Deep in his gut, he had a feeling that knowing her actual name was going to be important to him. He entered the room, dropped his clothing case on the floor next to the bed, and gently placed his computer bag on the little desk. He locked his door, plugged in his phone, and headed for the shower.

He had a presentation to give on day two and had plans to meet up with several colleagues tomorrow for brunch. After ordering a sandwich and soup that he asked to be left at the door, he threw on a pair of lounge shorts and waited for the light meal as he flipped through the channels on the TV and wondered about Oakley. She gave the impression that she was well composed, but her hands had shaken, telling him it was as much an act as anything else. He was very observant when it came to the opposite sex, and his protective instincts kicked into gear when he saw what he had today.

He hoped she was okay and had friends at the conference. He would try to check on her if he saw her this week. It would help him to put the incident behind him, and then maybe he could quit worrying about her. Right now, he couldn't stop wondering why she was attending the conference. Did she have someone to take care of her? Would she take more precautions for her safety?

The knock at the door alerted him to his meal's arrival, and after wolfing down the food, he was again wondering about Oakley, her blue eyes and fearfully determined but furious face when he came up to her and her attacker. Ryker admitted his best friend made a living in protection, and sometimes his cases bordered on mercenary. Their group of friends was militant about taking care of their own, which must be why he was so concerned about Oakley. He would check up on her tomorrow. It was his last thought before oblivion overtook him.

Chapter 1

The room was packed. The expectant energy was vibrant. Ryker straightened his tie and confidently glanced at the sea of expectant faces filling the temporarily converted ballroom. Dozens of attorneys, civilian law enforcement, mental health professionals, and military personnel had gathered for the annual Military Law Conference. However, his hands still trembled with nerves to be standing before them as the day's keynote speaker.

He'd not seen Oakley on Sunday and had assumed she'd been with friends or had stuck close to her room. He hated that he had not connected, but tried to push off his concern. And he definitely was not going to allow the thought that something might have happened to her to blossom. He dealt in facts, and the fact was, there was no evidence she hadn't decided to sleep in or do a final bit of work before the conference started.

Yesterday, he'd gotten a glimpse of her from across the room, and she had seemed recovered. Not kidnapped, or worse, then, and not missing the conference. All these things should have settled his mind and his gut, but they didn't completely. Mentally shaking off the feeling that something was off, he looked away and cleared his mind of everything except his presentation. Mostly.

Ryker reviewed his note cards for what felt like the fiftieth time, resisting the urge to tweak another point before scanning the assembled crowd with enigmatic gray eyes. He straightened his suit jacket and took a deep breath, letting it out slowly, as he had learned years ago, to calm his nerves. The weight of expectation was palatable.

A firm hand slapped him on the back. "On in five. You ready, mate?"

Ryker shook his English buddy's hand. "I don't know why you always seem to rope me into these things, Chris, but I'm ready. When this is all over, you owe me a drink, at least."

"You know you wanted to share. And I get you to do things because you're such a soft touch. I'll buy you two drinks. Time for me to do my bit and introduce you."

Ryker chuckled at the truth of Chris' words. What had actually happened was a bit different. As a successful attorney and former military man, the conference committee had invited him to speak at this professional conference on military law. After earning his law degree, Ryker had spent twelve years in the Army. Those years had included three combat deployments as the field JAG officer weaving his way, delicately, through Middle Eastern law as it pertained to U.S. personnel.

Now, at 40, he owned a thriving law practice with two junior but up-and-coming attorneys serving civilian and military clients. Ryker knew well that the achievement, so early in his career, was impressive. To a man like Ryker, public speaking should have been second nature. But standing at the podium, with the spotlight shining in his eyes, Ryker's mouth went dry, and his hands felt clammy. This subject was important. His intro was done, and Chris had started the applause. Ryker stood at the podium after shaking Chris' hand. He waited until the room quieted.

"Good afternoon," Ryker began, his voice resonating throughout the room.

There was a ripple of unease in the far right of the audience, and Ryker stopped speaking to re-assess the area. He could see several of his military friends were in different stages of rising and heading for the skirmish. Ryker had to control his desire to step into the fray as well.

In the far corner of the conference room was an uneasiness, then what appeared as a scuffle, with chairs falling over, a subdued shriek, more murmurings, and then someone ran from the room. If he was reading the situation correctly from where he stood, it appeared that the person who ran off had caused trouble for one of the women at that table.

Ryker was a fixer by nature, and his first instinct was to go to that far corner and make sure that everyone was okay, especially the woman who showed the most distress and looked in his direction as though he were the answer to her problem. Oakley. Damn, he knew his gut wasn't leading him wrong. He mentally talked his feet into staying in position at the podium and watched as Oakley appeared to reassure those around her.

In the midst of dealing with the issue, there was little doubt that Oakley Addison sought him out with her eyes. He interpreted her entreating expression as one of embarrassment, some fear, and something else. She was asking for his help. Something settled in him, and he knew there was more to their connection than mere friendship. He just knew it.

His logical side disagreed. Don't be ridiculous, his brain told his heart. But something about Oakley drew his attention and kept it there. As a fixer by nature, he could see that several people associated with the conference were addressing the problem, and he thought the best thing he could do was to carry on. So he did. But something in his gut told him to at least acknowledge that something was going on, as much for the audience as for Oakley, who glanced up again while speaking to the conference personnel.

"Well, it appears that whatever has gone on in the back corner of the room is being dealt with appropriately, so let's give them some privacy and go forward."

Funny that he felt compelled to say those words when he wanted to do anything but ignore the situation. He pushed those thoughts away, reminding himself that it was not his business, and he was not asked to intercede and continued with the speech.

"Today, I'd like to discuss some of the legal challenges faced by our brave men and women in uniform. Whether it be military or a first responder, there are pitfalls when they are faced with professional or personal needs that influence their professional worlds. They are a special group of people who have servant hearts. Issues often include civilian law enforcement and mental health providers, at a minimum. Despite that service and sacrifice, military personnel face unjust barriers to healthcare, legal counsel, and stable life after their service ends. As attorneys, as citizens, we have a duty to advocate for the men and women who have given so much. I'm talking about military members, but we could be discussing any of our community first responders who have had traumatic work-related issues and have stepped away from their service jobs in ways other than retirement."

As he warmed to his subject, his eyes connected with the audience, exuding confidence and authority. It was a subject that often twisted his gut, but he tried to channel his powerful emotions to increase his passionate pleas.

A rumble of approval rose from the audience. Ryker's nerves eased, replaced by the heat of his message.

Ryker noticed Oakley listening with great interest, sitting at the same far back table. He wanted to bring her forward, in front of where he was standing, so he could keep an eye on her. Oakley was beautiful, and his thoughts stuttered. He forced himself to look away from her to keep himself on track. Focus, Bennett. He cleared his throat and gripped the sides of the podium, knuckles whitening.

"I've dedicated my life and my career to serving those who serve our country."

"Furthermore," he continued, "the lack of legal representation available to our troops is a disgrace. They risk their lives for our freedom, yet we often leave them to fend for themselves when they return home. For some, it all works out, but the road to recovery and integration is long and bumpy for others. It's our duty to ensure that they have the support they need to reintegrate into civilian life or return from a traumatic event."

He continued to advocate for a different way; for compassion, understanding, and more robust responses that would help not hinder those who could not ease back into life as seamlessly as hoped. The rumble swelled to applause. Ryker stood taller, confidence surging within him.

"Together, we have the power to enact genuine change. Become a country that supports its veterans without compromising those who have kept the home fires burning."

The room thundered with applause. A fire had been lit within them, and together, they would blaze a trail to a better future for military men and women. His work was only just beginning.

Ryker stood at the podium finishing his presentation on military personnel, the military justice system, and how it could better interface with civilian law enforcement and the mental health community. He hoped to encourage better communication and better working relationships with civilian authorities.

"Thank you all for being here today, ready to effect change."

As the crowd erupted into applause, Ryker acknowledged their appreciation with a nod and a humble smile. He felt a deep satisfaction knowing he had impacted this attentive audience. As Ryker finished the question-and-answer portion of his talk, he locked eyes with the brunette that he just could not get out of his mind and determined he would check in on her as soon as the opportunity arose. If it took too long, he would produce that opportunity.

Somehow, he finished the last bit while continually seeking her face between each sentence to see how she accepted it. She was enchanting, with deep blue eyes that stood out and grew even more opulent against her royal blue blouse. There was something vulnerable in her expression but also a healthy dose of grit.

He finished and gathered his notes while the room applauded. Ryker looked one last time, and Oakley's smile dazzled him, nearly blinding him. He needed to reconnect with her, if only to satisfy his concerns about her and to prove she wasn't a gypsy casting a spell over him.

Seated near the back of the conference room, Oakley watched intently as Ryker spoke fervently about the challenges military personnel faced. As a psychiatrist specializing in PTSD and other mental health issues affecting soldiers, Oakley felt a deep connection to his words and found herself completely captivated by his passion. She knew that wasn't the only reason she felt a pull toward the handsome professional. He'd been her rescuer, but even more, she felt drawn to him.

Oakley's striking blue eyes met Ryker's piercing, stormy gaze for an elongated pause, making her heart race and her breath quicken. She felt a twinge of excitement deep in her core. She knew that flip-flop in her belly signaled her attraction. She recognized the feeling as attraction, something that had been absent for some time. It pleased her that Ryker was the one to awaken this sensation within her.

If it were residual feelings of hero worship, she was in trouble because she could not stop watching him or looking for him. She'd run into him several times over the last few days, but she didn't think he noticed her. If he did, she couldn't tell.

Sitting towards the rear of the conference room, Oakley observed Ryker with keen attention as he passionately discussed the obstacles that military personnel encounter in different arenas. What she whole heartily approved of was that he then included first responders in the same category of unmet needs.

She wanted to spend time with this man, have intellectual conversations, and explore her suddenly overly juiced libido. She had never had such a volatile response to a man before, and it scared her as much as it intrigued her. With Ryker, she fired on all cylinders of her being. She tried not to worry that it might be too intense.

The applause signaling the end of Ryker's presentation echoed through the room, and Oakley knew this was her opportunity. Taking a deep breath, she rose from her seat and made her way toward him, her petite frame weaving through the crowd of people who had clustered around the towering, broad-shouldered attorney.

Despite her diminutive build, she managed to weave through the crowd and approach him gracefully. To Oakley's delight, Ryker appeared to have sensed her presence before she reached him. He seemed to sense her presence before she made herself known; looking past the man in front of him, he made eye contact with her.

The hidden depths of Oakley's blue eyes, eyes her best friend told her held secrets yet undiscovered, briefly met Ryker's mesmerizing gray stare, causing her to feel an excited flutter deep inside. She twirled a strand of her hair between her fingers, an annoying and often unconscious habit that had developed as she grew up. Why did this make her hesitate and feel like a schoolgirl at her first Sadie Hawkins dance?

She was a psychiatrist, for heaven's sake, and she had no need to second guess or predict the outcome. Logically, they had a common ground to meet on, and if he wasn't someone she needed to continue knowing, so be it. But if he was even half of what ran through her mind, well, there was no way she was passing up that opportunity. She didn't want that 'what if' question to haunt her.

Oakley softly interrupted the discussion during the first lull, saying, "Excuse me, Mr. Bennett?"

Ryker diverted his full attention towards her. His intense facial expression seemed like he was devouring her while acknowledging her presence. He was intelligent, that was clear enough, but something else about him relaxed her fears but intensified her awareness. Much like the teens she occasionally fostered told her clearly, this was as confusing as hell. Emotions and thoughts that were unexpected would put anyone into the awkward category. At least, that's what she told herself.

She said, "I just wanted to express my appreciation for your speech, Mr. Bennett. You're creating an impact. One that is desperately needed during these stressful times."

He smiled. "Ryker, please. And thank you, Ms. Addison."

With a hint of nervous excitement, she reiterated, "Ryker. Please call me Oakley. I primarily focus my practice on aiding military personnel and first responders afflicted by PTSD and other psychological roadblocks to living a fulfilled and happy life. Adding first responders to your message was brilliant and timely. Your unwavering commitment to helping them holds a special place in my heart."

She knew their conversation was formal, but she needed to test the waters with this man before revealing her interest in more than his civic passions. Besides, they were at a conference where they had met over the apprehension of an almost assault. He could be a creep, but she'd lay odds that he was anything but.

As Ryker's warm hand gripped hers, Oakley felt a shiver run down her spine while his deep voice murmured, "I appreciate it." He then noticed her badge and asked, "You're a psychiatrist? It's good to know my message connected to you. One never knows if you are only speaking lawyer or if it translates to other professions and disciplines."

"It resonates and echoes with so many of my colleagues and my experiences.

Interest flickered in Ryker's eyes. "I know this sounds crazy, and if it spooks you after the other night, I get it, but do you want to go out with me? Maybe we could discuss this subject and others over some good food once today's sessions are over?"

Oakley's cheeks were ablaze with heat, and her heart skipped a beat. She peeked up at Ryker and noticed a glimmer of desire in his eyes that mirrored her own. "Sure, that sounds great," she said.

Her heart skipped a beat at the sight of Ryker's smile. "There's an amazing Italian bistro in the vicinity. A colleague of mine introduced me to it yesterday, and I'm eager to go back. I'd love to share it with you," said Ryker.

Ryker gave her a wry smile and said, "Today's meetings end at four, so meet in the front lobby at six? Is that enough time?"

"More than enough. Thank you. I'll see you then."

Oakley took one last look in Ryker's direction and met his gaze before he tipped his head as though to promise he would be waiting, and then they both resumed their conference day.

The conference day had several people who wanted to stay around and carry on further conversations, and the day extended well into the following hour, making it 5 o'clock before Oakley reached her hotel room. Deciding that the most important thing to her right now was to reconnect with Ryker Bennett, she decided to race through a shower, keeping her hair dry. She picked out the only outfit she had brought with her that was not too casual, yet dressy enough to go on what might arguably be considered a date.

Is that what she wanted to call this, a date? Why yes, yes she did. And if she were to be on time, she needed to pick up the pace. She still had her emails to check, her messages to go through, and a call to make to her assistant to ensure nothing was missed.

Once Oakley got into her client's information and needs, she, as usual, lost track of time and soon found herself running just on the edge of late. Grabbing her handbag and shoes, she snatched the key card from the side table by the door, slipped out, and let the door shut behind her. Sprinting to the elevator, she slipped in just before the door closed behind another guest and smiled apologetically to the guest as she slipped on her shoes, smoothed her hair, and ran her hands down her slacks to give them one last encouragement to lay flat.

When she stepped out of the elevator, she looked expectantly for Ryker and didn't immediately see him. Oakley then heard his deep voice coming from beside her and breathed a sigh of relief.

"It appears our timing is in sync. I feared you would be one of those early arrival people, and since I am an on-time or running a little late person, it might have been the start of a disastrous evening." He tipped his head to the side again in acknowledgment and appreciation. "And now we can both relax because neither one of us was late. Shall we?"

Offering his arm, he invited Oakley to loop her hand around the crook of his elbow. She did, and a sudden wave of electricity traveled up her arm, sending shivers down her spine. Now, that was a new reaction that was both worrisome and exciting. She wondered what else would be in store for her as she learned what other things this man was passionate about and what it would be like to be the object of his ardor and obsession.

Chapter 2

Ryker checked Oakley's footwear and grinned when he saw her confused expression. "I thought we'd walk, but I had to make sure your shoes were okay, or we'd have taken my car."

"I usually wear flats or low pumps because I'm one for comfort. And I didn't get in my gym time, so walking is nice."

Walking out of the hotel side by side, his hand easily slid to the small of her back as he switched sides and walked on the outside of the sidewalk. She noticed, but it appeared as though he had acted unconsciously because he kept on talking. It spoke to who he was, and though she wanted to compliment him or point out this positive character trait, she was loath to say anything to make him overly conscious of his actions. She would learn so much more this way. Once again, she had the tingling impression that this could be the beginning of a magical journey that would change her life forever.

Ryker started the conversation with comments about how busy Dallas was and the warm autumn weather. Then he moved on to discuss the one subject she wanted to avoid. "What happened this morning just before my presentation?"

Oakley paused as he opened the door to the restaurant that turned out to be just blocks from the hotel. Before she could answer, they were greeted by the hostess and shown to a quaint table in the restaurant. Ryker pulled out a chair for Oakley, the soft candlelight casting a warm glow around them. The Italian restaurant buzzed with energy, but at their intimate table in the corner, it felt as though they were in a world of their own. As Oakley took her seat, Ryker couldn't help but notice the delicate curves of her face, illuminated by the flickering flame.

"Thank you," Oakley murmured, her eyes meeting his before she looked down to peruse the menu.

"Of course," he said, his voice softened by the atmosphere.

After sitting, she steered the conversation naturally away from the early morning disruption.

"Wow, this is so nice. Thank you for bringing me. The atmosphere is like those in the neighborhood eateries in Italy that I would visit after college."

"I've been in Italy, but doing military business, not for vacation. I didn't get much time to see the sights, and I regret that."

"I was in an exchange program for my master's and learned about psychiatry in a handful of European countries. It was a great choice because it fueled my thesis when my Ph.D. program rolled around. It was lovely and an eye-opener. The families were incredible and showed me so much of how they lived. Something I won't ever forget."

As Ryker and Oakley ordered dinner, their conversation flowed easily. As they sipped on their glasses of red wine, the conversation turned from professional to personal. Oakley shared her love for hiking and her passion for photography, mentioning how she often found solace in nature while capturing its beauty through her lens. Ryker listened intently, appreciating the vulnerability she displayed and the joy that lit up her eyes as she spoke.

"Nature has a way of healing, doesn't it?" Ryker mused aloud, recalling his own experiences finding peace during long runs in the mountains near his home.

"Absolutely," she agreed, nodding thoughtfully. "It's amazing how the simple act of being outdoors can help us regain perspective."

"Okay, you've had enough time to relax, change the subject, and order your meal. I have a feeling you would like to pretend this morning never happened, but it did. What was the noise all about?" His demeanor spoke loud and clear that he was not agreeable to her ignoring his question.

"Bossy much?" she said. His lifted eyebrow said he was not taking the bait. She sighed. "Unfortunately, it was my fault. I have a new assistant, and she has run business offices, which is mainly what I hired her for, but she didn't have much frontline experience, mostly backroom organizing. I didn't tell her not to disclose more than I was out of the office and when I would return."

"Ouch. Did she tell one of your clients?"

"Worse, because they would have just called me. No problem because my phone is off during sessions, so they expect to get voicemail. Evidently, she mentioned it to a parent of a child who was in an emergency placement for foster care. I tried to push it off as a case of mistaken identity. He was looking for his daughter's social worker and thought it was me. I'll never know why he would have mistaken that, but it was a little unnerving to know he must have come from Kentucky to here."

"Not good at all. I don't like it. You have been accosted twice in almost as many days. Oakley, something isn't right here. How did you handle it?"

"I told him to leave, or I would call security, which the staff did anyway. I also told him he was mistaken. I even had to pull out my business card to prove I wasn't a social worker. I told him to contact the social worker on the phone and make an appointment if he wanted to tell them anything, but I was the wrong person." She shrugged. "Anyway, I'm sorry that I disrupted your presentation."

"I'm not. It allowed us to have this dinner and get to know each other. That can't be a bad thing. I prefer to consider it fate."

"Still, the timing was unfortunate."

"Not a problem. Thanks for making my presentation more memorable." He sat contemplating momentarily before asking, "Does it happen often? In your line of work, I can imagine things getting dangerous."

"No, but it does happen. I'm trained to deal with many of presenting issues, so that's a plus. I also have an emergency button I can push if needed, but I have only used it once. Also, not all of them know I have their child in therapy due to their placement."

"So you treat children and adults." It was a statement.

"I do. PTSD and traumas happen to all ages. I don't see children under five except on special request."

"You should be careful. You must understand how highly suspect it is that you were accosted twice in a town that isn't yours."

"Understood. Can we change the subject now, please?"

Her hopeful expression made him smile. "Of course. I apologize. I'm known as a barracuda in the courtroom, and I tend to forget I don't need to sink my teeth into every issue."

Dinner arrived, steam wafting off plates piled high with pasta and fragrant sauces. As they enjoyed their meal, Ryker shared his interests and tried to entice her to share hers. He recounted tales of his travels and the adrenaline rush he felt when skydiving. As he spoke, he could see the curiosity and admiration in Oakley's eyes, igniting a warmth inside him that had been dormant for so long.

"Sounds like you're quite the adventurer," Oakley said with a playful smile. "I've always wanted to try skydiving, but haven't worked up the courage yet."

"Maybe I can help with that sometime," Ryker offered, his eyes never leaving hers.

The woman was intelligent to a fault. Logic wouldn't get her anywhere when there was an unbalanced person before her, and that fucking bothered him. After giving himself a pep talk that she wasn't his, he found himself reciting; she isn't yours, she isn't yours. He was already thinking, what if she was?

"What safeguards do you employ?"

Oakley scrutinized Ryker briefly before putting down her fork and leaning forward slightly. "You aren't going to let go of this, are you? It's important to you."

"Correct, and it should be important to you," his demeanor was expectant.

She nodded. "I have taken self-defense classes, and I participate in an annual refresher course. I also have a panic button linked to my receptionist and building security. And before you suggest it, a weapon in my line of work could easily become a disaster."

"Understood. Where is your panic button kept?"

"Where is it kept? My desk."

"Won't help there. You need to have it in your pocket or around your neck."

"I think around my neck would be a bit obvious, wouldn't it? And if I am trying to engender trust, that would scream distrust."

"Not if it is part of a locket or something with the mechanism in the back of it."

"They make those?"

"Jewelry? Yep. I can have one made with that and a tracking device so that not only would you be able to say you were in danger but also where you were."

"That might have helped in the garage."

"It would have indeed. So think about it. I can help find one for you. I have an inside track."

"Ah, yes, your friends."

He nodded. "My friends."

"I'll think about it."

His mind went back to what he would absolutely require if she were his, and it was becoming increasingly obvious that she was going to be his. He would just bide his time and make the most of their connection here in Dallas. There was so much more he needed to know about her life.

It took a few moments for him to refocus on his dinner partner, and he was greeted by the sensual sounds of enjoyment that nearly had him climaxing. He shifted the subject back to the conference. It was time to change the direction of his thoughts. He reached over and poured her more wine as he asked a question.

"So, how did you end up specializing in treating veterans?" Ryker asked.

"And first responders. My father was career military, Army," Oakley said. "I saw firsthand the challenges soldiers face when they return home and how little support there is for them. I wanted to help in any way I could. My brother is a policeman, and my sister is a dispatcher in a small community for both fire and police. When Dad retired, he moved over to volunteer firefighter, and so, as they say, the rest is history."

"And the fostering?"

She smiled. "One of my passions. I do emergency placements, mostly. I don't always have a roommate, but sometimes, I do. Another reason I try to stick with mostly adults but why I can't turn down a youth dealing with trauma."

Ryker nodded and smiled. "I can understand that. Intelligent and compassionate, a winning combination." He grew somber. "My father was also military. He struggled with PTSD for years after his service. If it hadn't been for a psychiatrist with your dedication, I don't know if he would have recovered enough to continue raising his family and being a good husband and father. It was a long, hard battle to find the right help. And I have so many friends and fellow soldiers that suffered the same challenges."

"I'm glad to hear he found help," Oakley said softly. She glanced up at Ryker, struck anew by the warmth and empathy in his eyes. "Why did you become a military attorney?"

"Similar reasons." Ryker's jaw tightened. "Too many good soldiers face injustice because they don't have proper legal representation. I wanted to advocate for those who have sacrificed so much for their country." He grinned as he leaned back in his seat. "Besides, I'm damn good."

Oakley's heart swelled at his words, but his quip at the end took the sweet factor out of his words. She had never met anyone with such a deep, personal understanding of this issue, and it made her comfortable around him. She trusted him.

"It sounds like we have a lot in common," she said.

Ryker smiled down at her, his eyes glinting. "So it seems. I'd love to discover even more."

Oakley's heart was racing at the hidden conversation. Over a creamy Italian dessert of hazelnut panna cotta for her and tiramisu for him, which they shared, they spoke of more mundane things such as work and leisure time.

"I cannot believe you like to fish," exclaimed Ryker.

"Why? I've been fishing with my dad since I was old enough to go. I'm a great swimmer, too. I scuba dive every chance I can sneak away." She grimaced. "Which has been once this year. Life gets so busy, and going alone; well, you have to have a buddy, and my bestie isn't a diver."

"Then how do you go?"

"My brother had come with me a couple of times before he got married. Otherwise, I just hook up with another single diver."

"Oh, that's not safe at all. You can't do that." Ryker said with conviction.

"I've done it plenty of times." Her tone was defensive.

Ryker shook his head. "Well, it isn't safe enough to continue that practice. Surely a partner could be found. I'll ask around with my good friends."

Oakley just stared at him. "Did you just tell me I couldn't do what I have done for quite a while without incident?"

He had the grace to appear a little sheepish. "I suppose that is what I did, but it isn't safe. Not with all the crazies in the world."

"Thank you."

"You're welcome. For what?"

"For showing that even when you don't know someone well, you still treat their welfare as important."

"But I meant it. I'm serious."

Oakley laughed before turning quietly intense. "I know you are."

He nodded. "Good."

As the evening wore on, Ryker and Oakley continued to share stories and jokes, their chemistry intensifying with every word exchanged. It wasn't long before they realized that this initial encounter was far more significant than they could have ever anticipated.

Ryker listened with rapt attention, asking questions and sharing details of his own life. They discussed their mutual love of classic literature and hiking and their passion for helping military veterans.

With each word they exchanged, Oakley felt herself falling deeper under Ryker's spell. He was charming, intelligent, and caring, showing a genuine interest in getting to know her. She hadn't felt such a profound connection with someone for as long as she could remember.

"Oakley," Ryker began, his voice low and filled with emotion. "I can't remember the last time I connected with someone like this. I don't want this night to end."

"Neither do I," Oakley admitted, her cheeks flushing with excitement and vulnerability.

When the check came, Ryker reached for it before she could. "When you are with me, I pay." Oakley shook her head. "Today, I won't argue, but if I invite you, I am paying. It is equal. Fair."

His hand covered hers, sending a spark of warmth up her arm. "Life isn't always fair. As you get to know me better, you won't argue about things that you aren't going to win. I give on plenty of things, but I don't budge on the things that show me to be a gentleman or that I just believe to be right. That is an assurance that you can count on. Besides, most women like me to pay for the meal, open car doors, have them sit on the inside of a bench, or at least let me sit where I can see any potential danger coming their way."

Oakley cocked her head to the side, as if to try to decipher him. She took in where he was sitting, that he had opened the restaurant and hotel doors, and walked between her and the traffic. Yep, he really did those things. She was falling for him faster than she was comfortable with, but harder than she had the will to resist.

"You do all of that? I didn't think men like that existed in this generation."

"Well, probably not as many as I'd like, but definitely more than you think. I can see your mind working, and I want to assure you this doesn't make me a controlling jerk. What it does is keep you as safe as I can while showing you how special you are. I'm a total consent-centered man. You say no, I'll stop, but I might ask why. You okay with that?"

Oakley noticed she was rubbing her belly as though it were unsettled. It kind of was. All her training worked toward keeping herself safe and arming her clients with tools to do the same. Her asshole alert was usually spot on, and she had relied on its accuracy for over two decades.

Everything in her said Ryker didn't ring any of those bells. In fact, he seemed to be genuine and sincerely believed he should do those things for the woman he was with. She would bet the man was exactly who he said he was, and wouldn't that be... wonderful?

Oakley's heart was racing in her chest. Oakley found herself captivated by Ryker's passion, insight, and quiet humor.

Being the professional woman she was, and loving the control it brought her; being single meant she was the one she relied on, no matter how exhausted or mentally stressed she was. She used her tools, was a yoga lover, and listened to relaxing or fun music to destress. She also was on her electronics for an incredible amount of time, working into the evening too many nights a week.

Oakley knew how and what to do to stay healthy, but it took time, and sometimes, no, often, she didn't have the energy or desire to cook that eggplant, so frozen pizza it was. She wasn't as safe in the little things as she could be, and the list was slowly growing in her mind. Things could be different if she had a man who respected her but made it his business to take care of her. And yes, maybe sometimes told her no.

The shiver that ran up her spine surprised her, and when she looked up into Ryker's face, he gave her a knowing look. Arrogant ass. The bag he held it all in was gorgeous, intelligent, passionate, intense, yes, but arrogant.

Ryker's smile softened. "Oakley, don't think so hard." Her name sounded intimate on his lips. "Would you like to continue our date over coffee tomorrow morning?" What was he asking? To stay the night? Meet her in her room in the morning or at the coffee shop downstairs?

Oakley hesitated, knowing she had an early video conference appointment with a client. This was a client who was in a delicate place in his therapy, so she needed to keep up the continuity, even from the conference. Not wanting the evening to end, though, "I wish I could, but I have an early video session with a client." At the flicker of disappointment in Ryker's eyes, she added, "I'm free for lunch, though."

He sighed; his regret was obvious. "I have the attorney luncheon tomorrow. I can do dinner, though, if you'd like."

Oakley grinned enthusiastically. "Yes. I'd love that."

Ryker squeezed her hand before releasing it. "It's a date."

"Anything you don't like?" he asked as they began walking home.

"Oysters, snails, cute bunnies, or vermin. Oh, or extremely spicy or exotic food."

"So no alligator or Asian Fusion, I take it."

"Uh, no, thank you. I'm not a fusion food fan. Sorry. But I might try alligator if they disguised it well enough." Her smile told him she really wasn't that interested in trying alligator.

"I've been surprised a couple of times, but I get it. TexMex work?"

"Yep, just so all the choices are not super-hot."

"They have a variety of heats, so I'm sure there is something you'll like, but we can go somewhere else if you like."

"No, I'm game. I guess I'm pickier than I thought," Oakley said.

"Hey, no. Don't do that. Be loud and proud about things you believe in or like and dislike. It helps me know more about you and helps me understand what you need and want. I'm not going to be shy about this, Oakley. I really like you, and I don't think that will change much as we get to know each other. And since we don't live too far from each other, I can foresee some weekends hanging out together."

"That might be nice. So dinner tomorrow night? Meet at the same time and place?"

"Put your number in my phone, and I'll tell you when I can get reservations. I know where we should go." She did, and then he sent her a text to complete the circle of information. His number included a business card. "Now, you can always find me."

Oakley didn't respond verbally, but nodded and slid her phone back into her bag. As Oakley walked to her room, she felt lighter than air. She had a date with Ryker, and the prospect filled her with breathless anticipation. After years of struggling to find someone who shared her values and passion, she finally met a man who understood her. No one else ever had. And he was flaming hot.

She couldn't wait until tomorrow. For the first time in a very long time, she could see herself with a man, making a life, a family home that included keeping her practice. Not too long ago, Oakley had considered starting her own family through adoption or artificial insemination. She had talked herself out of it for one very important reason; she hadn't given herself enough time to go out into the world and see if she could find her soul mate or someone close to that description.

That was one reason she had decided to frequent more seminars and conferences, to find another professional who would understand her love of her career and her business and what a delicate balance that would be. She feared she was being unrealistic when she wanted not only another professional with the understanding of how much running a business and her career took, but also her driving need to have a family. But there had to be someone who attracted her that also wanted the same things in life.

In her limited but oh, so vivid experience and her vicarious living through colleagues, men often wanted everything in their favor. They expected women professionals to stop working, or reduce the significance of their job, to raise the family. The man in the relationship, of course, kept his career and advanced with little day-to-day involvement in the nurturing and raising of the children unless his job allowed him to be at home and during family vacations. That was not for her.

Another area that Oakley had seen in friends' and colleagues' relationships was the need for the woman to swallow her ideals and control and cede it over to her husband or a significant other. Evidently, tradition was the main reason, and another was to bring harmony in the home because men had more delicate egos, though, according to her sister, delicate was being kind. Oakley smiled when she thought of Ryker being characterized as having a fragile ego or a fragile anything.

I wonder if he has ever thought of having children. Okay, a thought too far, Oakley. Enjoy him while you are here, but things are too busy once you're at home. He has his practice, and he is likely to have a hectic life as well. His description of his work was vague, but he had done a good job of getting her to talk, which was usually her superpower. Yes, Ryker Bennett was indeed someone to take notice of. Her libido sure did.

Chapter 3

The next morning, having finished her virtual appointment and rushed through the last of her morning rituals before leaving to attend the conference, Oakley ran down to the coffee shop to order a large coffee and grab a blueberry scone.

"A large caramel latte and a blueberry scone, please."

"Never mind the lady's order. I've ordered for her."

Turning toward that deep, masterful voice that made her weak in the knees, Oakley asked, "Did you? How did you know?" He smiled, gesturing for her to exit the line.

She shrugged, waved at the barista, and moved out of line, leaving a tip in the jar.

"Were you there when we were talking last night?" There was amusement on Ryker's face.

She accepted her coffee and reached for her pastry. "Um, yes?"

"Then you will remember that you said your guilty pleasure was to have a caramel latte and a blueberry scone every workday. In fact," he said as he led her to the conference room, one warm hand placed in the same spot as yesterday, "you put in your fancy machine to make your own at work because sometimes you come in too early for the coffee shop. How did I do?"

"Embarrassingly well. You have also reminded me I haven't worked out for days. I'm going to hurt when I go home and start up again."

"Swim," Ryker said as he leaned into the door to the conference floor.

"Swim?"

"Yep. Easier on your body but works the muscles so you can quickly get back to the place where you can work out without hurting."

He led her to a table and slid out the chair for her. Without a glance around the room to see where her psychiatrist posse was, she sat in the offered seat. Several people of assorted professions were sitting with them within a few moments. Ryker seemed to be a popular guy because he introduced her to everyone as they wandered over to the table. Only one was an attorney. There were military and law enforcement, a fireman, and a physician, all acquainted with Ryker.

She took a long drink of her now cooling latte and another healthy bite of her scone, her little sounds of enjoyment making Ryker's cock twitch. That would not do here in the middle of a large crowd. He could not sit with a napkin over his lap all morning. He leaned over and spoke in a low, serious voice.

"When we are in public, it would help me greatly if you could eat silently."

She grinned, and Ryker continued with a warning. "I appreciate all your adorable sounds of enjoyment, but only when we are alone. I am already going to have zipper teeth imprints on my cock."

She responded innocently. "But the blueberries are so fresh, and the flavor of sugar, lemon, and slightly sweet bread; I mean, how can I not enjoy it?"

"I'm glad, but just know that there are consequences to your actions. Some are good, and some are ouch-y."

"Ouch-y?"

"Yep, as in my hand on your luscious backside for teasing me into an uncomfortable state."

She licked her fingertips of sugar and then held up the place where she had just taken a bite.

"I don't mean to cause you pain. Would you like a bite?"

"Minx. Remember, you have been warned."

Ryker carefully rearranged his cock, giving her a final cautionary lift of the brow before leaning over to speak to the person sitting to his immediate left in an effort to redirect his thinking and, hopefully, his inflated dick. Her quiet chuckle had a distinct giggle quality that was nearly his undoing. When was the last time a woman's enjoyment of food or his discomfort did it for him? A very long time. He wanted this woman badly.

He noticed that in a couple of seconds, Oakley had changed from carefree and teasing to a psychiatrist who grappled with real-world issues every day. She was like a drug, and he was fast becoming addicted to her. The morning's presentation was well done, and the rest of the day, with breakouts and disciplines meeting to discuss how to address the varied views of the collaborative work needed for a better outcome, was something that Ryker enjoyed.

He occasionally spied Oakley, who seemed in her element. He texted her the time to meet him in the lobby, taking the opportunity to check in with her to make sure she was enjoying herself. She replied she was and was excited about dinner this evening.

He was taking her to a little dressier restaurant, but nothing more than business casual. He caught her eye once, mid-afternoon, and using a dip of his head and communicating with his eyes, he checked in with her. She smiled and nodded slightly. She could even read his body language—this woman.

He was sitting in the lobby when Oakley strolled off the elevator, relaxed with a spring in her step even though he knew she had been "on" since early that morning. He stood and reached out his hand, kissing her lightly when she approached with a smile.

"You have more energy than I would have thought by now."

"Full disclosure?"

"Always," said Ryker as he led her to his car the valet brought around.

"I left partway through the last session because I knew if I didn't get a nap, I wouldn't last through the dinner. A two-hour nap worked like a charm. I highly recommend it."

"Skipping out for a nap so you can go out with me? I approve." Oakley laughed, and he helped her into his car. "The naughty woman at my table this morning, though, was asking to be punished."

"Oh," she said nonchalantly as her face grew pink.

He was glad the sun was still up so he could see her cheeks change color. He'd like to change the color of another set of cheeks. His mind went to what taking her to his bed would be like. He wasn't in any doubt it would be heaven. He slid into his seat and waited for her to buckle before slipping into early evening traffic.

"Oh, yes. This naughty young lady was trying to cause me to take an unscheduled trip to my room."

"How dreadful," said Oakley, her amusement evident. "It has to be annoying when those sudden, unexpected distractions pop up." She slapped her hand over her mouth to stifle the chuckle.

Ryker's surprised laughter came in a burst of mirth. "It was, and I have yet to deliver the little minx's punishment, but I will. Soon."

"She must be one lucky girl."

"We'll reassess later, after her punishment."

The moment he said it, Ryker could feel the silence fill with sizzling need and desire. How could he want this woman so badly when he had only spent a few hours with her? It didn't matter because when you know, you know. She. Was. His. To save him from going caveman dominant and turn the car around to take Oakley to his bed now, Ryker forced the conversation toward more neutral topics, but the casual, comfortable demeanor continued throughout dinner and dessert.

"I love a woman who eats dessert if she wants it. I can't tell you how many have turned down the offer or have tried to eat off my plate instead of ordering their own."

"So you don't like people eating off your plate?" asked Oakley as she spooned another bite of her raspberry and cream sorbet.

"No, that isn't it. I am fully into sharing if I offer you part of my meal or dessert. But when you do not order a full meal or dessert and expect me to share mine, nope. The issue is consent."

"Good to know."

"So, Oakley, the question is, what are you consenting to?"

Chapter 4

What was she consenting to? Good question. What was on the table? Oakley had never connected to a man like she had connected to Ryker. But why? He was open about being bossy, harbored some antiquated thinking where men and women were concerned, and was unapologetic about any of it. And for some crazy, hormone-induced reason, she got chills of lust when she thought of him.

Why not have what would equate to a weekend fling? She would return to her office on Monday morning, and deal with medication adjustments and other people's problems. And an empty condo. So, what was the harm? None that she could see. She'd asked around, and those who knew him gave him high marks in the decent guy category. Yes, it was risky, but sometimes, calculated risks are worth it.

"Just what are you offering that would need my consent?" she asked quietly but with obvious interest.

"Oh, sweetness. I have so much to say to that question, but I'd say, first, we could go to my room or yours and see how personally compatible we really are. If there are enough sparks, we could try out the bed. It's early enough in the evening to figure out many answers to unasked questions. Are you willing to take a chance?"

"I'm not interested in forever, so I want you to know that going into this," said Oakley.

"How about we don't worry about that and just learn to enjoy each other? The rest will take care of itself."

"Ryker,"

"Oakley, trust me not to go too far but just far enough."

"Alright."

Oakley was amazed at how quickly Ryker got the attention of their barely conscious server, paid the check, and had her strolling outside to wait for their vehicle. She'd almost not finished her dessert. She knew he was eager to see where this could go, and so was she. Her imagination had already taken flight.

She wondered if she would be attracted enough to go down on him, but Oakley knew she wouldn't allow him to go down on her. It was different for a man than a woman, even if it shouldn't be. He had to be all into her, and even then, it might not be enough enticement. For women, sucking cock was fun, except she didn't swallow. It wasn't her thing, and no one had complained.

Was she as intimidating as some men had said? Maybe she shouldn't even experience this crazy hookup because she liked Ryker and didn't want to lose him as a friend. She turned in the seat, surprised she was already inside the car. And how did she get the seatbelt on?

"Oakley, stop. Whatever you are thinking, worrying about, or have had to go wrong in the past, that is not us. If you pull out a butcher knife and start jabbing the air, I'll be pissed and likely not want to continue, but if you don't intend on doing that or something similar, we'll be fine."

Oakley gave him an incredulous stare. Then she said with calm assurance. "Well, fine. If you intend on taking all the excitement out of the evening, we can go the boring route."

Ryker nodded. "Yes, let's do that for at least this first time. After that, we can negotiate."

She gave him a sigh, and her countenance grew comically pouty. "If you say so."

He laughed, and she joined in. They pulled into the hotel parking garage, and Ryker helped her from the car. "So, yours or mine?"

"Yours. I can return to my room if I want to later."

"But you won't want to. I can almost guarantee it."

"We'll see, Romeo."

He shook his head vigorously. "Oh, not Romeo. I think I prefer Rhett Butler or even Mr. Darcy. Surprised?"

"Hmm. We'll see."

OAKLEY HAD CHOSEN TO dispense with all the politeness like wine and chat once they entered Ryker's room. She pulled him down to her and kissed him. Ryker didn't disappoint. He met her eagerness with his own. She started the connection, but he quickly took over control. She nipped his lower lip. Their tongues collided and tangled. Ryker landed one light smack to her backside.

"Behave, little hellcat. Get these clothes off. You won't need them for a long while," he said as he stripped at lightning speed.

Oakley stared at his fit body. His chest and belly were taut and well-defined muscles moved when he did. So that's what rippling muscles looked like in person. Her hand moved forward to lay her palm on his pectorals with the full intent of moving them slowly down his defined muscles. One would never know that this masterpiece of manhood lay under his suit and tie. A sharpish slap landed on her ass, and she squeaked in surprise.

"You need to listen, sweetness. I said strip."

"But you are so gorgeous."

He smiled in a smirking way. "I can see I need to help you. Mind me now; touch me later."

He began to remove her clothing as she looked down at a stupendous cock. She didn't usually remember much about a guy's cock once they broke up, but man alive, this was a perfect specimen. She licked her lips as she absent-mindedly started to take off her bra, and he groaned.

"Earth to Oakley. Finish stripping, baby. If you're good, I'll let you touch."

"Mmm," was all she said, but she finished undressing.

He flicked her breasts, rolling the nipples between his fingers, and she moaned before realizing she stood naked in front of this man who was bossy and attentive. He was already wreaking havoc with her mind and body. How could she only have him for a few days and not be forever damaged at the loss?

Oakley thought for one quick moment about stopping before they went any further. She wouldn't be so devastated after just getting naked, but if they played and consummated, that would take her past the point of no return.

"Oakley, whatever that negative thought was, you are to disregard it. Do you want to be here with me?"

"So much. Probably too much."

He nodded. "Me too. I see you and feel you. I want you. I won't die if you don't stay, but I'll hate it." He waited. "It will be painful."

"I feel the same way. It's like if I don't explore this, I'll always regret it. I don't like regrets."

"Same. Climb on the bed so I can explore your sweetness. We both want this. We both crave the other, and I find I have to experience you to prove you are a mirage in my desert-dry life."

She had one last hesitation, knowing that if she went forward, nothing would ever be the same again. Without giving that thought any deeper consideration, she crawled onto the bed and sat on her bottom cross-legged, waiting for Ryker to direct her.

"I don't want you to think I let people dictate to me. I like to be my person and make my own decisions, so just in case you think this is who I am, this is who I am with you tonight, but don't get used to it."

"Noted, now hush." his lips landed on hers softly at first and then became more insistent.

When Ryker's hand slid down her stomach to the top of her pubic bone, Oakley sucked in her breath. The warmth of his touch raised the heat of her core, and she gushed. She arched as he continued his descent into the drenched channel of her sex.

She drew in a deeper breath. Ryker watched her gaze focus on the ceiling as he brought her to the edge of ecstasy. Her eyes rolled back as she lost herself to the moment. Her eyes closed in ecstasy as she rocked against his body, the pleasure of his touch infusing her with warmth and energy.

HER LIDS FLUTTERED, the only sign of the orgasm that was about to erupt within her.

While his fingers swirled inside of her, he had to taste her.

"Mmm, so good, sweets. You taste like the most decadent honey."

He returned to her clit as she moaned with each flick of his tongue. Ryker smiled against her folds. She must like dirty talk because she gushed again, her clit growing larger with the pressure of his sucking. He moved his mouth down through her glistening folds, and his thumb traveled up to her now abandoned clit. Suddenly, she froze before uttering a low, almost tortuous moan of release.

Oakley's earthy musk was all over him, but this was different. The smell of her sex engulfed his senses, filling his head with her aroma, the scent of her arousal. And he needed her. Her moans were low in the back of her throat, husky and deep. They were sexy and soft, and he loved they were only for him.

Ryker leaned back on his haunches, grasping his cock; he rolled on the condom he had thrown on the bed earlier.

"Ryker…" came the plaintive plea. "I need you more."

"Good, sweetness, because I am coming in. Are you ready?"

"Hurry," she urged as she tried to grasp his cock.

His growly voice gave her a warning. "Uh-uh." Then he notched his cock head at her slick opening and slid in slowly but persistently.

Oakley tried to take him faster by arching her pelvis. A stingy slap to the side of her buttocks stalled her movement, and he finished entering her.

"That was naughty. I will have to finish that punishment tonight because you are racking up the transgressions."

Then the talking and playing were over. Ryker pounded into Oakley as she smiled, then frowned, then moaned her need to climax again. He changed angles, and when he found the right one, the one he knew would put her over, Ryker hit it every time he entered and withdrew. Her hand clenched and unclenched, grabbing the bedding beneath her and holding on tight.

He changed the angle again and drove deeper. Leaning down, he ravaged her lips and moved down to suck and tweak her nipples before falling back for the grand finale. Once again, his girl froze, and then, instead of moaning, she cried out her release just as Ryker grunted his last few thrusts into his own release.

"Damn," she panted.

"Hot damn," he answered. "That was so damn hot; you have ruined me for anyone but you."

"Good," she murmured as he kissed her.

"Got to get rid of this condom. Be right back."

When he returned to the bed, he found her sprawled over the side nearest the door, and her light exhausted snores were adorable. He cleaned her up, not knowing if she wanted it, but it was gentlemanly. If he had his way, someday soon, it would be his come dribbling down her thighs, and he would want her to keep it all inside in preparation for his baby. It would likely be considered macho, or self-centered, or egotistical, but Ryker didn't care. As he looked down on the beauty, he knew, without a doubt, that she was his, and he wanted his babies in her belly, her lips on his, her in his bed every night.

He gently rolled her over to the interior side of the bed. He slept between the door and her. He climbed in bed with some lounge shorts on just in case she wasn't into morning wood. Spooning Oakley felt right. It all did. He was going caveman again and keeping her. He hoped she quickly agreed, or he'd have to work his strategy out to make it happen, but somehow, some way, he wanted her with him, forever.

Chapter 5

Over breakfast three days later, Oakley passed her plate with the remainder of her meal over to Ryker. "I don't know how you can eat so much and not gain weight."

"Muscle burns more calories."

She grinned mischievously. "Are you saying I'm fat?"

"Nope, and I'm not easily drawn into dramatics. But, at the risk of starting them, I'm saying you need to exercise more. We'll work on that once we're back home."

"I'm too busy," she said dismissively, startled that she laced her words with a pouty flavor.

He lifted his brow but didn't comment on her change of tone. "Oakley, you have to take better care of yourself. Beginning with eating well and finding an exercise routine you enjoy."

"But I exercise. I just can't imagine enjoying it," she said defiantly. "And I eat."

"When you remember. Sweetness, I haven't seen you step into that gym once since you've been here. And I see how you lean toward junk because it's what you're used to. Quick and easy."

"You haven't been with me the whole time. Besides, I haven't seen you work out, either."

"True. Likely because I'm in there a little after six every morning. So when did you use the machines?" asked Ryker as he scooped up the last of her scrambled eggs.

"I went inside the next morning after I got here."

Ryker noticed she wasn't meeting his gaze. He put down the fork and caged her chin with his hand. "And?"

"And it was busy. I went for a walk instead."

"Okay. So when did you use the equipment?" Oakley tried to tug her chin away, but he wasn't allowing her to go anywhere. "Eyes up here, Oakley."

"Okay, fine. I haven't, but I have walked all over this hotel, and I'm on vacation. I shouldn't have to sweat if I don't want to."

He chuckled. She was a little bit defiant. He loved that about her personality, but sometimes it worked against what was best for her. He'd planned on being around to help with that. "Agreed. How about at home?"

"Oh, I have my universal and treadmill."

"Nice. Used how often?"

"Evidently, not enough. I'm not a muscle monster. I'm not interested in competing in an Iron Woman competition."

He lifted his eyebrow at her and shook his head. "You tend to be a brat when not happy about being under scrutiny. I believe that is avoidant behavior. Am I right?" She avoided his eyes only giving his observation credence.. Ryker leaned over and kissed her. "Baby, you are gorgeous. Show-stopping, but something must be done about your unhealthy habit of disregarding your physical needs. Maybe swimming or tennis will add in some enjoyment and exercise."

"You're like a dog with a bone."

"I learned it from my best friend. He gets things done. Now, quit diverting the focus of the conversation."

She leaned back in her seat and sighed. "You're probably right. I love riding horses, but I haven't had any chance to do that in a long time."

"I know where some incredible horses are stabled. We'll figure things out. So, when we return to Lexington, we have some catching up to do at our practices, and then I want to see you. So, how about Wednesday night dinner and Friday night sleepover?"

She laughed. "A little old for that, aren't you?"

"Oh, no. My sleepovers are strictly adult rated and only with you. The games played at my sleepovers are rather naughty." He wiggled his brows suggestively. She laughed again. "Now I need to head out, and I know you do too. We'll meet tomorrow night for an early dinner, say five-thirty or six, at the All-American Café, so I can make sure you made it home in one piece. Sleep in tomorrow. It will make falling back into your routine easier if you are well rested."

"I like that café because it has North, South and Central American food. It's the only place I know that serves fried sweet plantain. Yum." She smiled and checked her phone. "Yikes, we need to get out of here. I'm stopping at my parents' house tonight, so I won't be back to my place until early afternoon tomorrow, but I'll sleep in."

"Text me when you stop and then again when you leave and finally arrive home. I'll call if I don't hear from you, and if I have to do that, there will be consequences."

"Incentive. But was it to remind me to call or not to call?"

"Minx. I'm serious about this. I will track down your parents' number and call them if you don't call me. Then your ass will definitely be sorry. And no speeding. I'm not high on patience regarding the safety of what's mine. And you, my dear, are mine."

Ryker had firmed his tone to bully his immediate hesitancy over too much too soon. However, he knew what he felt. He also was beginning to realize that Dr. Oakley Addison was not one to curtail her experiences merely because of the danger factor. Not that she walked into danger head-on, but she definitely courted it with her choices, and that was something that drove Ryker crazy. How was he to keep this woman safe if she didn't heed the awareness she possessed? She simply disregarded it as not enough of a concern. For a psychiatrist, it was unexpected.

Oakley's parents lived south of Bowling Green. She lived in Versailles near Lexington, and Ryker lived between Georgetown and Lexington. It was a twenty-to-thirty-minute drive between them, but not bad. Meeting in the middle, like at All American Café, helped lessen the trip.

Oakley gave him one of her discerning psychiatrist's looks. "There is a lot to unpack in that, but I won't test the waters yet. I'll text when I arrive, but remember that Friday afternoon traffic might be heavier than either of us expect."

The goodbye that Ryker and Oakley had shared when they finally parted was still fresh in his mind, but this time, he wasn't willing to take any chances. He walked her to the car, said goodbye, then watched her drive away until she was out of the lot before getting into his car.

Oakley had already become very important to him, and he decided to keep a close eye on her. He knew she needed extra assurance in some areas of their newly declared relationship, and she hadn't outright rejected the idea of having a family together—which was an absolute must for him. However, she expressed her fears of becoming so busy parenting that she wouldn't be able to maintain her career as a psychiatrist—which worried him because her job was not less important than his.

There was so much about Oakley that said forever, but he knew there were areas where she needed more reassurance. They hadn't had much time to talk, only during the last few evenings, so it was very early days, but he knew that while the hours they spent this week hadn't been much, it had cemented their desire to try. They also both acknowledged that talking while at a conference was easier. It flowed uninterrupted, unlike life back in their real, heavily scheduled life.

Oakley had communicated her fears of being so lost in the job of parenting that she didn't maintain her practice. That she might even want to put her job on hold for her family, and that was something she felt unacceptable, especially at this stage of her career. Ryker did not point out that one changes as one continues on with life. Our priorities, desires, and goals all change as we do, but he kept his own counsel. It was something they could talk about later. Much later.

Over dinner the following evening, they finished the conversation, and Ryker left Oakley with another thought to occupy her mind concerning them. "Right now, we are both heavy on the side of career, but either of us might curtail our jobs at some point. We might want to work fewer hours, do daycare at work, work from home, or make any number of adjustments."

"Oh, I forgot about all those alternatives. I guess we can work that out. I was so focused on the 'build my practice' scenario, the alternatives never entered my thoughts."

"An additional, important thing that I'm looking at is if we don't have children. Hell, sweetling, we aren't even married, engaged, or exclusive yet. Not that I am not ready for exclusive, because I am. But don't try to run all the races before we get to the starting gate."

She gave him a sheepish look. "You're right. I don't know why I'm hung up on that one aspect, but I am. Exclusive, huh? Can we pend that for a bit?"

"Of course. But you should know that I am going to be exclusive, regardless. I can't date two women at the same time."

"Good to know. I'll be too busy for more than one guy, but I want to reserve my decision. I was only going to have a conference fling, you know."

"But I won you over."

"You did." Her smile was brilliant, with a touch of shyness.

Ryker hoped that meeting and getting to know Jac and his other friends, and seeing how their lives were full-steam ahead, even with children, would be a great help.

Wednesday dinner that week didn't work out, as Ryker and Oakley found themselves deep in their work catching up. A case Ryker was working on had suddenly cracked wide open, and striking while the iron was hot seemed prudent. But they talked every night just before going to sleep at ten-thirty. It was close a couple of times for both as they tended to bring their work home, but they had agreed. On Friday, they met for their first sleepover at Oakley's. They talked as they sat relaxing on the sofa.

"It seems hard to pull away and make time when I'm deep in research or writing notes. I haven't had to stop until I'm ready, but after the last week, I'm finding that while we won't be together except weekends, I am more rested because I have to be ready to sleep by ten-thirty," said Oakley. "I hope that timeline doesn't extend to our weekend because I'm sure we will be

"So that has helped you create better habits. I like it. I told you I was good for you, and we would be good together," bragged Ryker. "I knew I was a workaholic, but I also get out of the office more times during the week than you do. I do a lot less one-on-one time with clients and more work behind the scenes. But weekends are not scheduled. We can stay up for as long as necessary." His suggestive smile was met with Oakley's shyly sexy response.

"You did tell me that, and getting outside more in a day might be a good thing as well." Oakley grew quiet.

Ryker drew her into his arms while sitting on Oakley's sofa. This was her weekend to host. He asked, "What's going on? You seem to be worried about some problems."

"I'm fine. It's just been a week. I'm mentally tired and having difficulty relaxing."

Ryker scooted around so he could massage her shoulders and neck. "Be still my heart," she said. "This might be better than sex."

"What? Absolutely not. When we're done here, I'll feed you and then show you just how wrong you are."

"I'm looking forward to that demonstration."

He kissed behind her ear, "Me, too."

Later that evening they validated the understanding that sex was explosive between them, but the connection went so much further than the physical. He needed to take Oakley to the heights of ecstasy to find the same release. All night the air was thick with desire as Ryker and Oakley shared their passions. The scent of their mingled sweat and the feel of tangled sheets around them seemed to fuel their excitement.

The taste of Oakley's lips on his was intoxicating, and her breathy moans in his ear sent shivers down his spine. They continued exploring each other's bodies, their connection deepening with every touch and caress. It filled him to have her in his life, and he believed that she felt the same when she shared her words of passion. They had a connection he'd never had before. Strong. Vibrant. Real.

Ryker couldn't believe how much he adored Oakley; his heart was so full of love that it felt like it might burst at any moment. He couldn't get enough of her, couldn't stop the overwhelming feeling of wanting to be with her for the rest of his days.

Each time he looked into her eyes, he felt like he was staring directly into her soul, seeing all of her beauty, her strength, and her vulnerability. And as they lay together in the afterglow, he couldn't help but feel like he had finally found his true soulmate. He wouldn't rush her, but Ryker knew that he'd found his forever in Oakley.

In the following weeks, Ryker and Oakley spent as much time together as possible, their attraction growing stronger with each passing day; whether in video chat, text, phone calls, or their weekend connections, it was becoming harder to go to separate homes.

There were days that Oakley had more to let go of than others. She said she had a few clients that made her earn her pay with them, but she understood her clients' needs and felt she met them. Fall was in full color. The air was brisk, and Ryker was antsy.

He decided it was time to make the pronouncement that not only did he want them to be exclusive, although they already were, he wanted her to wear his engagement ring, but one step at a time. He wanted them to wake up every day together.

"I want us to be exclusive and for us to move in together."

Oakley was quiet for a moment. "I have a two-bedroom condo that would not accommodate you, and your place isn't much larger. We won't fit. Besides, I'm near my practice, and you are near yours."

"Okay, let's get one somewhere between, and it won't be more than fifteen minutes either way. I'll sell my flat and find us a larger one. Then you can sell yours, and we will consolidate."

She kissed his eager lips. "Exclusive, done. Can we wait a little on the moving in part?"

He lowered his forehead to hers. "Oakley Addison, I love you. If you want to wait, I'll wait, but I'll be at your place during the week, and you can be at my place on the weekend. I must be close to you every evening and send you off every morning. Say yes to that."

"You love me? Already?"

Ryker nodded, then pulled her in close, kissing the top of her head, his arms wrapped around her. "I've loved you for a while, but I didn't want to scare you off, and I wanted to sit with the realization for a bit. You are it for me, Oakley."

"You're it for me, too. I wasn't sure it was long enough to have these feelings, but I've never connected to anyone like I do with you. I think the living arrangements you just described work for me right now."

"Good." Ryker kissed her sweetly. "We have been invited to my best friend's house tomorrow evening. They are celebrating another good business year. I want to bring you to the fun."

"Do you? Will they like me?"

"Oh, sweetheart, they will love you. Jac is already saying if I don't bring you tomorrow, he and Sharlee, his wife, will crash any private party we have."

"But he wouldn't, right?"

"Oh yes. They both would and likely bring the gang and their significant others with them. Best to get it out of the way on our terms than theirs."

"It rather seems it's theirs, anyway."

"Jac likes to get his way."

OAKLEY'S GOOD FRIEND Bella was included in the invitation, and Oakley drove Bella to Ryker's place. Bella, a bubbly and vibrant woman with sparkling eyes and an infectious laugh had been Oakley's friend since college. They had a few moments of alone time in the car on the way to Ryker's.

"So I haven't seen much of you lately. Is Ryker my competition now?"

Her friend laughed, but there were times that Oakley wasn't sure whether she was serious. Bella had moved to Lexington when Oakley had decided to open her practice here, leaving a lucrative paralegal job with a large legal firm. Oakley had tried to talk her out of it, but Bella wouldn't hear of it.

When Oakley had vetoed moving in together because she liked her privacy, Bella had been sullen for a while, but before long, she was living several streets over. Boyfriends came and went with Bella, and Oakley's boyfriends were few, very few. Ryker was different.

"Yes, he is part of the reason why I'm busy, but not completely."

Bella play pouted. "Guess I'll need a boyfriend until you have finished with Ryker."

"That's just it, Bella. I think Ryker is my forever."

"What?" Was that panic in her voice? "You're too young. And you haven't known him long enough."

"This feels different, Bella. Very, very different."

"You aren't suddenly moving in or anything, are you? You love your condo."

"No, we aren't moving in yet. But we are having sleepovers. The workweek is at my place; the weekends and holidays are at his."

"Oh, guess you don't need me around if you have him, then."

Oakley could hear the hurt in her friend's voice and tried to alleviate the worry. "Sure I do. Ryker wanted me to invite you and a date tonight. He said if you were my best friend, then you should meet his best friends. No reason we can't expand our friend circle."

"Hmm. What do these people do again?"

"Lots of things, but I'll let Ryker explain on the drive over."

Bella was quiet most of the way to Jac's except to ask Ryker about the people they expected to meet.

"Okay, so there is Jac and Sharlee with their son Storm who's about a year and a half. Jac owns the security agency, and his wife is part of the tech team. Then Garrett and Callie. Garrett is part owner, and Callie is his wife, who is also on the team. They have their pre-adoptive placement, Danica. Monroe and Mallory, she is a pharmacist, and he is on the team. Mark and Jessie, he is on the team, and she is the agency accountant. They have a newborn, Anora."

"Wow, that's a crowd."

"And there is more. Kaden and Ivy, he's a team member, and she is a martial arts instructor. I'd like you to take defense classes with her, if you would, Oakley. It couldn't hurt."

"I'll talk to her about it. Bella, you could go too. You were worried about not us getting girl time in."

"Sure."

"Okay, where was I? Oh, right, there is Carter and Becky. He's on the team, and Becky is Jac's personal assistant and office manager. Then there is Finley, Storm's nanny and a prior Marine, who is single. Levi is also on the team, a prior Marine, and is also single. For now."

"So, are you on their team, or do you work for Jac, too?"

"I'm the agency's and Jac's attorney. Not one of his team members, but we are all family. Many of us are prior military. It's a bond. Jac has a family he works with, and one of the women in the family is a therapist. Like me, Jac keeps her on retainer for his Alpha team and the other two teams he has. It's important to have mental health back up."

"It really is," agreed Oakley. "Wow. Is this Jac's place?" she asked as they approached the manned gate.

"Holy shit, this is huge."

"It is, but Jac isn't like what this property implies. He is intelligent and won't be fooled, but he is also generous and ferocious about protecting his business, employees, and everyone he considers family."

"Wow, Ryker, you picked well when looking for a friend," said Bella.

"We hit it off in college and stayed close through military service and now in the civilian world."

THE EVENING WAS FULL of laughter and getting acquainted. Dinner was the most fun Oakley had experienced in a long time. Oakley tried to remember everyone but was sure she didn't do it. The delightful seafood feast was cooked and served outdoors in an extensive patio area with heaters to keep off the growing chill as the night descended.

Bella was one to make friends quickly, so it was no surprise when she seemed to settle in quickly. It took Oakley a bit longer, but the group was so inclusive Oakley didn't take much longer than Bella to feel included.

So, twenty people, one precocious five-year-old girl, one adorable little boy, and a newborn little girl attended the party. Storm lasted through the meal before his mother, Sharlee, took him to bed, returning with a monitor some minutes later. Every thirty minutes, either Jac, Sharlee, or Finley would go up to check on him. Someone said something about notes but nothing else.

Oakley blushed more than she had thought possible, but the teasing was good-natured and not distasteful.

"Thank goodness you're a shrink. Ryker has always been just a tad off."

The women took her and Bella, who was making eyes at Levi, aside and gushed over her and Ryker.

"I knew the man had taste, but you were better than we had hoped," said Ivy.

Mallory said, "Ivy, filter, dear."

"I don't know why people keep telling me that. Kaden says I'm just an open book, and I figure everyone else is too. I try to think before speaking, but honestly, I don't know what I'm saying wrong."

"Well, keep trying, dear. The good thing is," said Callie dryly, "if you do upset the wrong person, you have the martial arts skills to stay safe."

"Oh, right, that reminds me. Ryker said you do martial arts classes. I don't know when I'll fit things in, but I'd love to slide into one of your classes."

"I'll work it out for you. I love new victims."

"Thanks, Ivy. Bella might come too."

"Right, where Oakley goes, I go."

Jessie laughed. "Well, not everywhere, I hope. Otherwise, I will have to reassess my opinion of Ryker."

"Uh, no. Not everywhere," clarified Oakley.

She could feel another blush coming on. These women. She had never had a posse, and with these women, that was more than possible; it was likely mandatory. It just cemented her need to be part of this life with Ryker. This group of professional, madly skilled men and women was who Ryker called friends and family. Ryker had a family, but it was a small tight group consisting of his mother, father, aunt, uncle, and two first cousins who were spread across the country. His parents and his aunt and uncle lived in Arizona. Not close in proximity, but Ryker called his parents every Sunday. She had started calling hers at the same time. They alternated who finished first. That made being with Ryker even easier. The man was made for her.

Evidently, Bella was comfortable too. She had stumbled to the door because she had had one too many cocktail concoctions of Callie's. Levi picked her up before one of the other guys could. He grinned.

"I can't get in trouble for carrying a single, unattached woman to the car."

But, if Oakley was right, there was one unattached woman in the room who didn't seem happy with the chosen method of transport. She had narrowed her eyes, and then they shuttered. Finley quickly said goodnight and went upstairs, assuring Sharlee she would check on her little charge. No, if Oakley wasn't mistaken, Finley was definitely upset. Bella needed to tread carefully, but if she stayed true to form, she would think that was a challenge. Oakley would try to stay out of it.

The next morning, after dropping Bella off, Oakley and Ryker bought groceries together like an old married couple, which made her heart settle. Yes, he was a high-powered, international lawyer, but he was down to earth. He was a little cocky, but she liked that because she was a little sassy, and that didn't seem to bother him.

"Ryker, I can't believe how lucky I am to have found you," Oakley whispered into Ryker's ear as they transferred the food from the cart to the trunk, her voice full of emotion.

"I'm the lucky one, sweets. I never expected to find someone like you," he replied. Oakley could hear and see how true that was for him. Happiness swelled her heart to almost bursting.

"Okay, let's get this loot home so we can start moving some of your things over for the weekends. Then I have a beautiful drive I want to take you on tomorrow, and tonight we will cook those gorgeous steaks we bought."

"I love you, Ryker Bennett."

"I love you too, sweetling. More than I ever thought possible."

THE FOLLOWING WEEK was going to be hectic, but on Sunday, knowing they would have a heavy week, he took her to his parent's summer home, even as autumn's hold was giving over to winter's frosty fingers. Climbing to the roof, the clear night lay before them, and it revealed an enormous sky, the perfect canvas overflowing with clear, bright stars.

"My dad used to take us up here to see these stars every chance he got. He even built this little landing with rails so my mother wouldn't worry. We would go camping, and he would tell us what we were seeing. That's when I decided Orion was my favorite constellation."

"This is so magical. Thank you for sharing it with me."

"I'll share everything with you. I've been waiting so long for just the right woman. Thank God I've found you."

Oakley sighed and snuggled in to watch the glitter show.

RYKER STAYED AT HIS house Thursday night, but he expected to see Oakley at five tonight. When she didn't arrive or answer her phone, he got an uneasy feeling. He sent her a flurry of texts but received no response. Doing what he wouldn't have recommended to anyone else, he took a drive, arriving at her office before it closed at its typical six p.m.

It was Friday, so the traffic was a bit heavier. Still, when Ryker pulled into Oakley's workplace parking lot, his anticipation mounted as he looked forward to spending another weekend together. But when he arrived, things seemed off. His mind raced with worst-case scenarios as he rushed to her office, finding the door locked and the lights off.

As he returned to the parking garage, he swept a glance over the area for her car. His brow furrowed when he spotted the car parked in its usual spot, seemingly undisturbed. All of his previous reasoning, why she wasn't where he expected, flew out the window. She wasn't just running late or forgot to charge her phone, or left it on silent. She didn't lose track of time. The possibilities were many, but almost none applied now. He moved his car next to hers. The garage was two-thirds empty.

He called the office and got the answering machine. "Strange," he muttered, feeling a sudden unease settle over him. "She should be ready to go by now, or at least someone should answer the office phone." His unease ratcheted up, and he had to sternly call his apprehension under control.

He stepped out of his car and approached Oakley's vehicle, noticing that it was locked and appeared undisturbed. His concern grew, and he pulled out his phone to call her again, and this time he was met with her voicemail. Maybe that meant it was on.

"Hey, Oakley, it's me. I'm at your workplace, but I don't see you. Give me a call back as soon as you can. I'm getting worried." Then he called his friend.

"Kaden, hey man, are you near your computer?"

"Always. What do ya need?"

"Can you track where Oakley is? You got her number?" He heard some clicking on Kaden's keyboard.

"Found her. She's driving. Why?"

"She isn't, not in her car, anyway. I'm at her office, she isn't answering, and her car is right next to me."

"With Bella?"

"Good thought. Hold on." He dialed Bella.

"Hey, tall, dark, and handsome. What's up?"

Without any fanfare, he blurted out, "Is Oakley with you?"

"No, should she be?"

"No, I can't find her, and my gut is clenching." Along with his muscles, mind, teeth...

"I'll call her. Hold on." Listening to dead air was ominous in his present mental state.

She came back on. "Nope. It goes directly to voice mail."

"Okay, thanks. I'll let you know when I find her. You'll do the same, right?"

"Of course."

He disconnected and reconnected with Kaden. "Can we track her?"

"No, man, her phone was just turned off."

"Damn. I didn't get that necklace for her, nor did I get Sharlee to teach her the Keep Safe program. It's going to happen as soon as I locate her. She isn't with Bella and didn't answer when Bella called either. It went straight to voice mail."

Ryker paced the parking lot, his mind racing as he tried to make sense of the situation. He texted her, hoping for a response, but it went unanswered. If her phone was off, nothing would get through. Where was she?

His panic mounting, Ryker sped over to Oakley's apartment. But when he let himself in with the key she'd given him, the place was empty. There were no signs of a break-in or struggle, but that only made the knot in his gut twist tighter.

It didn't make sense. None of this made sense. Oakley would never just disappear without a word. She wasn't the type to stand him up or change her plans last minute. No, something was very wrong here.

He retraced Wednesday night, all good. They had made slow, gentle love before falling asleep in each other's arms. Thursday morning, she was in a hurry, but her mood had been up. She grabbed an apple and a pastry, which he grumbled about good-naturedly because she had used the treadmill for a few miles before showering and heading off to work. They had talked on the phone last night at ten-thirty like always. They had spoken after court this morning. They were happy. Content. No, it wasn't because she had changed her mind or was irritated with him.

Ryker knew, deep in his gut, that Oakley was in danger. And if no one else would help, he'd have to take matters into his own hands. He would search every inch of this city to find the woman he loved, no matter what it took. He wouldn't stop until Oakley was safe in his arms again.

"Where are you, Oakley?" he whispered under his breath, his heart pounding with dread.

Chapter 6

Garrett and Monroe sat in Ryker's living room, watching him pace. "Don't wait to make the call. You know how these things are. You must be proactive, and can't be alone while we are looking for her, so you always have an alibi. You were always on the screen, so you obviously didn't take her or hurt her."

"Shit. You're right. I need to stay above suspicion so I can find her."

Monroe added. "One of us will stay with you. Now make the call."

Monroe and Garrett encouraged him not to wait for the reasonable time to report her missing. Making that call was the hardest thing he had ever done. His insides were being torn apart, and he was helpless for the first time in longer than he could remember.

Ryker's heart pounded as he gripped his phone, calling the police to report Oakley missing. His voice nearly broke at one point before he took a deep breath and continued. But the officer who answered sounded unconcerned.

"I'm sure there's a reasonable explanation. She probably just had a change of plans and forgot to call you."

"No," Ryker insisted. "That's not like her. She would never do that." But the officer didn't seem to believe him.

As the call ended, Ryker ran a hand through his hair, panic and frustration churning inside him. He had to find Oakley. He couldn't lose her, not now, not when they'd just committed to building a future together.

Then Sharlee called, shattering his slowly decomposing thoughts, and asked for a video meeting, and he realized he wasn't helpless. Help he had. Direction is what they needed.

"Let's do it."

Immediately, Becky came online, bringing in each team member individually, until the screen was lined with smaller snapshots of his friends and their significant others. Nearly everyone was there.

"I appreciate this, guys. I hope I've overreacted," said Ryker.

Jac nodded. "I'd have been pissed if you hadn't called. This is what friendship is all about, and in this room are men and women who are family of the closest kind. And," he smiled, "we've got skills."

Ryker was so glad they did. He could physically get through the mess, but Jac and company had equipment that made it more efficient and, occasionally, fun. This was serious, though. Fun would come after he had his Oakley safely at home.

"Police said they can't do anything for forty-eight to seventy-two hours. They said she is competent and don't deem her a risk. They expect her back at work Monday morning. According to them, she's not going to just take off."

"Which means this is serious," said Ryker, stopping his pacing to speak.

"They believe since she has a practice, she'll be back Monday. The marine I often work with on the force gave me some things to eliminate over the weekend if she doesn't return. It will get them further down the road if they do deem her missing. I can call back on Monday if she isn't back then, and her car isn't moved."

Becky nodded. "What are they?"

"Well, checking everyone she knows or would come in contact with. So I called her parents, and they haven't seen or heard from her since the normal call on Sunday."

"Right," said Sharlee. "What else?"

"Checked with Bella, who says she hasn't talked to her in a few days and has not seen her since coming here last weekend."

Monroe leaned forward and took the center screen next. "So we need a plan. Sharlee, I know Ryker doesn't know her complete name, but Oakley has an office manager/receptionist with the first name of Shandra. We have to talk to her. Then there is the trace that Kaden could do of her cell before they turned it off or it died. Get us the map of that area."

Mark added. "We also need to tap into the cameras in that building and the parking area."

Jac came on screen. "Carter, will you and Levi check out the garage and building? See what there is that we might have missed. Add cams wherever you can see we need one. Her office for sure, and her car will need one."

Carter nodded. "We got that."

Jac paused before continuing. "Kaden, you're on IT with Charlotte. Let's see if Oakley's bank card or any of her cards have been accessed. Then, we can trace the time and approximate leads through the city. We have CCTV, but we aren't wired like London, so it might not be as helpful if she leaves town. Becky is info central. She'll compile and distribute information as it comes in. Questions?"

Garrett nodded. "I'm sticking with Ryker, I guess. Monroe is returning to you to begin strategizing the information we have now and later get."

"Good," said Jac. "Stay at Ryker's house, and we will put surveillance on Oakley's place. She's one of ours now, and we will bring her home."

"Thanks, everyone." Ryker's voice was sorrowful but determined.

That was Friday night. Saturday and Sunday stretched agonizingly long.

Sharlee called a conference call on Sunday afternoon. "Okay, check in. We'll start. Tracked the cell to the loop, Highway 4, and then on Highway 27 toward Paris."

"She would have had to drive past you then," said Garrett.

"She would have indeed, but I don't believe she was driving. Her car is in her office building parking lot," said Monroe.

"There are a shit load of farms out there. And land." Mark pointed out the obvious, but Ryker needed all the information he had to process correctly.

"There is," said Jac. "So we had to expand."

"She has been having stalkers or creepy stuff happen to her before we got together. It's how we met, actually. When I had just arrived in the hotel's parking lot, she was yelling for help as she fought off an attacker. It happens in her line of work, but this person seemed random. Thinking she was an easy target.

"A few days later, a parent of a recent foster child she was seeing decided that she was the social worker for some reason. Possibly they weren't satisfied with their child's treatment and followed her to the conference. The police will have to get the information on those two."

Garrett said, "Write down everything you can remember about that and share it with the police tomorrow when you make the official report."

Carter spoke. "Levi and I went over the area and found nothing, so we tagged the car for sight and sound. Then we tricked the office door to alert us to her office door opening and her outer door opening."

Levi added, "Checked her apartment, nothing. Did you say you spend weekdays there, Ryker?"

"I do, but Thursday, I didn't. I had a case in court at eight am Friday that I was still working on and needed to be fresh the next day. But we talked that night and during the day on Friday, after court. She seemed fine. She wanted to grill that night." He sounded tortured at the memory.

"Okay, well, that all fits what we found. She had takeout for one, and it looks like nothing else spectacular happened after that. We left cameras inside and one for the walkway outside. The parking is already covered, but only the police are given access. Let's leave that to IT."

Kaden nodded. "Got it covered already."

"We have gone over the footage, and I am waiting for my program to work to get into the office building's system. Meanwhile, we are still going through cams, but we aren't sure when she left the building until we get through to the office manager. We found her, but she hasn't answered her phone, and when Carter went around, no luck. She was gone for the weekend."

"Could Oakley have gone somewhere with her?"

"No way. She was thinking of firing her to get a replacement. It wasn't working out."

"You don't think Oakley sacked her and Shandra lost it?"

"Shit. I didn't think about that, but no, I really don't. Garrett and I are checking out the area around her car and the car again. See if we missed anything."

"Keep us informed," said Monroe.

Ryker climbed out of his car with Jac and Sharlee on the video on his phone. "It's getting colder, and she doesn't have her coat. I saw it in her car. She isn't someone to wear one, but she does get cold."

Ryker stood in the dimly lit parking garage and thought they should put more light in here. He hadn't noticed that before. A cold gust of wind ruffled his hair as he scanned the area for any signs of Oakley. His heart pounded in his chest, and fear coiled like a serpent in his stomach. He clenched his jaw, frustrated by the lack of progress in their search.

"Get out of the cold, man. When you file the missing person's report, that will add our friends on the force and get us access to the office building. Sharlee and Kaden are still working on it, but for some shit reason, something is blocking them in real-time." Jac sounded frustrated and concerned.

"Damn it!" Ryker cursed under his breath.

The high stakes of waiting the weekend after Oakley's disappearance weighed on him like a thousand-pound anchor. He couldn't bear the thought of losing her—not when they had only just begun to explore the depths of their connection.

Garrett encouraged Ryker back into the car. "Sitting out here will do no one any good. We need to go in and make our plan for tomorrow morning because at seven am bright and early, you will be making an official missing person's report, and then we will be at Oakley's office figuring this out."

True to his word, the next morning, Garrett went with Ryker to make the missing person's report, and at eight, Sharlee, Callie, and Carter met Ryker and Garrett at the office. Garrett and Levi made Shandra hesitate, her eyes widening as she took in the men. However, after Ryker explained, she apologized for not being available over the weekend and unlocked Oakley's office.

"Won't the police get upset about this?" asked Shandra.

"Maybe, but we have waited all weekend to get in here, and if it makes you feel better, cancel her appointments. I'll take the flack if she returns this morning."

"Yeah, like she will complain about anything you do. I think you are the only one she would allow to go through her office. She trusts you."

"Have you seen Bella or anyone else come to visit her in the last week?"

"Bella came on Tuesday and tried to get her to go to lunch, but she had a 12:30 appointment. Bella was grumbly but seemed to be okay when she left."

"Thanks, Shandra. Do you have any surveillance cameras in here?" asked Sharlee.

"Sorry. Oakley won't allow them. Patient confidentiality. I believe there are some in the hallway, though."

Just then, Kaden sent a message. "I got into the surveillance feed. Downloading last week's through today."

Sharlee read the text and smiled. "No worries. We'll let the police handle that."

Ryker pivoted from his spot to get a broad view of the area. "It might be a few days before they contact you or as soon as today. But I filed a missing person's report, so someone should contact you sometime soon. Do you mind staying today if she doesn't come in?"

"Sure. If we don't hear from her, should I close until we do?"

"If you don't hear from her or me, cancel this week with her clients and stay home. I'll make sure you get paid for this week. Do you have an extra key for the office?"

"Oakley does in her desk. A spare for both hers and the office's door." Carter headed for the desk.

"Talk to me about clients," asked Garrett as he watched Carter methodically gather information from the office.

"Funny you ask about that. I was going to mention it earlier, but..." she shrugged. "She had some kind of altercation in the office with the last client, and then she left early."

"Who was it?" asked Callie.

"I can't tell you that. But it was a new client. She disagreed with Oakley and left in a huff."

"That's suspicious," said Ryker.

"It's happened before. Sometimes people think psychiatrists are just going to write prescriptions rather than do some therapy and counseling; of course, that's not how it works. The people get mad, and they leave."

"Then what happened," asked Garrett.

"Then Dr. Addison... Oakley said she was going home early at about 4:20, something about grilling, and said I could go too. So I left a few minutes later."

"Did you see her in the parking area?" asked Garrett.

"No. I didn't see anyone."

"Okay, thanks," said Ryker. "I'll keep you updated if you give me your number. I'll give you mine."

"Oh, I have yours. Oakley made sure I knew how to contact you."

Ryker input Shandra's number in his phone, took one last look around and followed his friends out. Sharlee was on the phone with Kaden as she pocketed the drive that she had used to copy information from Oakley's computer. She also grabbed Oakley's computer bag and filled it with all the bits of paper she found in and on the desk. Under the blotter pad was a list of passwords, all but the last one crossed out. She'd have to have a talk with her when this was all over.

"Wait!" Shandra called out, holding up her phone. "I got something here. Bella, Oakley's best friend, just sent me a message saying that Oakley told her she needed a break and would be back in a week."

Sharlee put her hand out as though Shandra would simply pass it over to her. When Sharlee showed no sign of backing off, Shandra reluctantly did. Sharlee sat in a waiting room chair and started working on things with Kaden on the other end of the phone.

As the others were working on things in the office, Sharlee snorted. "Except it wasn't sent from Oakley's phone, and the message to your phone wasn't from Bella's phone. Someone is playing blind man's bluff around here."

"What?" asked Ryker. "This doesn't sound right. Not like her."

"Not like Oakley, or Bella?" asked Sharlee.

Ryker frowned, skeptical. He knew Bella had her eye on him, and he couldn't help but wonder if this was another one of her games. "Did she say anything else? Like where she went or why?"

"Nothing specific, just that she'd been feeling stressed lately and needed some time away."

"Are you sure it wasn't from Bella's phone?"

Sharlee passed the phone back to Shandra. "Nope. It isn't, and I'd venture a guess that someone piggybacked the internet link."

Ryker shook his head. "I don't know about these things, but shouldn't that mean we need to get over to her apartment?"

Sharlee shook her head. "Won't help. You don't have to be in their living room to do it."

Ryker looked at Sharlee. "Maybe you should explore where it came from. Because who would know Bella was Oakley's friend and use those names from different phones? It's too odd."

"Happens all the time," said Sharlee, her face hidden from Shandra. Her facial expression belied her words.

Ryker played along. "Okay, you're the expert." Who the fuck had his baby girl, and who the hell did he have to maim and destroy to get her back?

With all the things they could gather that might help them find her in hand, they headed to the security offices with one more mystery added to the mountain.

Chapter 7

"It doesn't make sense," Ryker said, shaking his head. "Why wouldn't she tell me? We were supposed to be exclusive now. Building a future."

"Maybe she didn't want to worry you," Callie suggested. "Or maybe she wanted to test your commitment to her."

"Either way, it doesn't add up," Ryker insisted, his gray eyes narrowing with determination. "Oakley wouldn't just leave without telling me. And what about this new client? It sounds odd that they disagreed so quickly, don't you think? There's too much that doesn't fit."

"True," Jac agreed, rubbing his hands together for warmth. "But we can't ignore what her best friend or someone else says. We should at least look into it. Might be a lead or a taunt which is a lead all by itself."

"Fine," Ryker conceded, his jaw tight with frustration. "But I'm not giving up on the possibility of foul play. Oakley means everything to me, and I won't stop until I know she's safe."

"Understood," said Kaden. "We're all here for you, Ryker. We'll find her."

Mark stood and said, "Think it's time you and I took a little trip to Bella's to clear some of this up."

Bella was nowhere to be found. She had taken the week off from work. It was beginning to look like she had met up with Oakley.

"Something isn't right."

"Agreed," said Jac.

By the end of the next day, all they found was that Oakley's cell phone was still turned off, and the last place it had sent a signal was the highway that first day. The message to Bella came after that, except if it wasn't Bella's phone that sent it, either Bella had two phones, which began to look very suspicious, or they cloned a phone and did that for Oakley and the person who sent that message was the kidnapper.

They would follow up on that.

"Her car hasn't moved," said Sharlee.

When she called Shandra about what she knew about the car, she said, "Sometimes Oakley goes for the weekend with a friend, and nobody thinks anything about it."

"And when was the last time she did that? I want to check to see where she went."

"You can do that?"

"Girl, I can do that in my sleep. Now when was the last time?"

"I think about a month before she went to Dallas?" Shandra was hesitant now.

"Got it. She left her car in the garage?"

"Oh, I assume so," said Shandra.

"Then how did she get to work on Monday?"

"Um, I guess her car? Look, I don't really know."

Sharlee and the gang knew Ryker was right. Things were too fishy, and the waters were getting murkier by the minute.

Something was definitely going on. And not just because they had a date the night after they decided to be exclusive.

"We'd even begun to talk about our expectations in a serious relationship. We specifically listed notification of the other partner if we were not going to make it home on time or if things changed. We promised to be open and honest with each other because that's the type of relationship we want." Ryker turned desperate eyes to Jac. "She's my breath, Jac. We have to find her."

The police called on him this morning and asked about their relationship. He was clear and calm but couldn't stop his voice from shaking when thinking about her being in danger.

"It's been a few days now. Maybe she'll show up soon."

"Five, it's been five days, and she won't just show up. It's been too damn long. I've hired a securities company to help. They are my closest friends and won't stop until we find her."

"What company?" asked the younger officer.

"Jacquard Reynaud and Associates."

"I hear they're good."

"They're the best. We'll find her."

"Just stay out of the police's way," said the more seasoned officer.

"The more people looking, the better. We will go where we think the information points. Jac said he'd share with you when they have something promising. Here's his card if you have questions for him or his team."

The more senior officer took the card, and both shook Ryker's hand. He knew they were doing their best, but with the restraints of laws holding them to the line, Ryker didn't have much hope of them coming up with any leads his friends didn't get.

By the time the following Monday rolled around, Ryker was beginning to show his lack of food or sleep. The team had reassembled to see if they could piece any more together. Jac was waiting for the notification from Shandra of whether Oakley had returned to work. They also called Bella, who still didn't answer her phone.

"I'm taking another run out to Bella's house. I don't know her family, or I'd call them."

Jac and Ryker went to her house with no response. Her car was still gone, and it appeared as though she hadn't returned the whole week. Garrett and Mark went to Bella's office. Carter offered, but his size worried some people. When there was no good outcome, they started on a hunt to find her. Jac and Ryker first went to the police to see if there was any update. They spoke to them daily, but this was another monumental milestone day. Unfortunately, it seemed Sharlee and Kaden shared more with them than they offered in return.

"I don't understand, what do you do next?" Ryker asked Jac's contact, Linden.

"I wish I could say there was much more. But we have her name and picture out as a missing person who could be in danger. Really, we will shake the trees, but nothing is falling out," said Officer Linden.

"Keep us informed, Linden. We appreciate your help," said Jac.

As they were climbing in the car, Ryker said, "I don't appreciate what they're doing if it doesn't produce anything. Fuck. We have to locate Oakley now. I have my juniors doing the calendar calls and the like, but I have a few cases to put my energy into, and I don't know if I can split my attention. I've sent in continuances and hope that flies for now."

"Something will give soon. I've got my guys scouring the community in places most of society doesn't want to know about. Sharlee and Kaden are going deep, and we will find her. This is the type of thing people talk about."

"I'm grateful for all you're doing. I'm just maxing out on my ability to be civil."

"Understood."

As the days turned into another week, Ryker was taking sleeping pills to fall asleep. "Shit, next I'll need pills to sleep, to give me an appetite, to wake me up, and help me shit. I'm falling apart."

Kaden updated everyone on their progress. "I've been checking street and business CCTV. The cameras were blocked and put on a loop, but it came off too soon. About ten minutes before Oakley came out, I could finally see a woman leaving her office. She arrived in the garage; her body language was angry, so probably her client."

"The woman stopped to speak to someone in a van parked next to Oakley's car. Then, nothing for fourteen minutes, then we see the back end of the van as it is in the process of completing its turn out of the garage."

Ryker's thoughts swirled like a whirlwind as they split up to pursue their respective leads. He had spent the previous days wondering if Oakley was really just taking a break, or had something more sinister happened? The uncertainty had turned to absolute certainty that something bad had happened to his girl. The reality that she may never come back gnawed at him relentlessly.

He recalled the warmth of Oakley's touch and how her laughter made his heart soar. He pictured her tender smile and how her eyes sparkled when they were together. They'd come too far to lose what they had waited so long to find. Sharlee called him a half an hour later, bringing him back to the moment.

"Burner phones, both of them."

Ryker put it on speaker for Jac and Garrett to hear. "So, not real," said Jac.

"Not real. None of it."

"Fuck! Someone is playing a cat-and-mouse game with us. Do they have Bella too? Should we tell the police?"

Garrett reasoned, "They know they can't find her and that she is Oakley's best friend. They know she hasn't shown up to work, either."

Jac stood. "We will find her, and if Bella is with her, find her too. But we do need to examine the possibility that she might not be with Oakley or knows where Oakley is and is riding under the radar for some reason. Charlotte, delve into Bella's background. Regroup meeting first thing in the morning."

"My juniors have all the cases and are continuing the big one I can't do right now. I'm all yours. Put me to work, or I'll go mad."

"Got it."

"Oakley," Ryker whispered into the night, the wind picking up around him as if to carry his words to her. "I won't rest until I find you, baby girl."

The next morning, on his way to Jac's office, Ryker took a detour and arrived at Oakley's office, hoping for any sign of progress. But the space remained dark and empty, frozen in time like the moment she went missing. The meeting they had this morning was brief.

Kaden represented the IT group today. "We are working on watching the CCTV trying to figure out which car might have been the one that Oakley left in. Also, trying to get a clear enough image for facial recognition on the woman patient."

The next morning, Ryker went back and opened up her office just to feel near Oakley. He sat at her desk and gazed out the window, watching the world go on as if nothing had changed. But for Ryker, everything was different now. The light had gone out of his world, and all that was left was the desperate need to find Oakley again.

His phone buzzed, and Ryker saw it was Sharlee. He answered immediately. "Did you find something?"

"We may have caught a break," Sharlee said. "There's footage of a black sedan in the parking lot around the time Oakley went missing. No clear shots of the license plate yet, but it's more than we had before. It left after the van."

Ryker's heart raced. "That's great news. See if you can enhance the footage and run the vehicle through any databases. We have to identify who was driving that car."

"On it. I'll let you know as soon as we have something." Sharlee hung up, and Ryker smiled for the first time since Oakley disappeared.

They were getting closer. He could feel it. Ryker left Oakley's office, eager to check in with Jac's team and review the case from every angle.

But when he arrived at his car, Ryker froze in shock. There, on the front seat of Oakley's car, was a single white rose and his business card. No note, no explanation—just a chilling message meant for his eyes only. Oakley had said she wanted white roses at their wedding because he loved a pure white rose. To him, it signified starting over, fresh, new. What the fuck?

His blood ran cold as the truth dawned on him. Whoever took Oakley knew precisely where to find him, and they were watching his every move. Since the police had verified his alibi by his home security cameras and then later with Monroe and Garrett, his office, and the events afterward, they had ruled him out as a suspect in about an hour. But spending time alone was tearing at his sanity.

He called Jac and let him know. Jac said, "Don't touch anything. Take pictures from outside. I'm calling Linton."

Linton arrived with another officer and a forensic guy. "Tell me what you're doing here, Ryker, and how you found this."

Ryker explained his trip to the office and sitting in Oakley's seat to be close to her and then checking her car for some unknown reason. "That's when I found this. I don't have a key to Oakley's car. She has a key to mine, but she was going to trade this one in, so I never took her spare. I have a key to the condo because we usually stayed there during the week and at mine on the weekend. I never thought about it, but her spare car key must be in her bedroom."

Linton nodded. "And the card?"

"Mine. Oakley had a few in the glove box, in her office, and in her purse. I have some in my things as well. We were cross-promoting each other as a couple would."

"Okay, and how about the rose?"

Ryker ran his hand through his hair. "I told Oakley that I loved simple, pure white roses. They symbolize fresh, new, starting over to me. Oakley said she wanted them at the wedding. See, we had just gotten engaged. We just had that conversation the Wednesday night before."

Jac and Garrett arrived in their SUV. Jac shook Linton's hand, and they discussed what was going on.

Ryker spoke again. "How could they know about something we had just talked about? How could they get inside her car? Fuck this is crazy."

"They?" asked Linton.

"The fuckers who have my Oakley. Are they trying to get at me? Taunting me? I have too many clients to count with enemies that became mine when I got them off their charges."

Jac had Sharlee on the phone. "Someone wanted you to see this, Ryker," Sharlee said quietly. "It feels like a message, an invitation to find her. We're getting closer. We'll find her. Let's go look at what we have with new eyes now. We are on the path now."

ANGER AND FEAR WARRED within him as Ryker made his way back outside to his car as the police left. He had to stay focused, and look at this logically instead of letting his emotions cloud his judgment. Oakley was out there somewhere. He just had to find her. He was going to review the more significant cases from now, and then work his way back.

Ryker pressed the heels of his hands against his eyes, dragging in a shaky breath. "Where are you, Oak?" he whispered.

Oakley heard something. It was thin, as if measured, a clock ticking; the world outside was louder than she expected. There was too much happening. She tried to focus on something, but her eyes couldn't make sense of anything.

That incessant pounding in her head. Did she have a fever? Her skin was cold and clammy to the touch, or was it?

The sheets on her bed were soft and cool. Her whole body felt like that usually, instead of rough. Hot. Why was it suddenly so hot? She was on fire. Her skin was hot, her body hot too, and she felt sweaty and disgusting. Her headache raged like a forest fire, and it hurt to blink.

She needed Ryker. He'd know what to do. He'd help her.

"I just want to go home to Ryker," she whispered. "Please come get me, Ryker. Please."

Chapter 8

Ryker awoke with a start, his heart pounding. For a brief moment, he thought he heard Oakley's laughter drifting through the apartment. Then her desperate pleading for him to find her. But when he opened his eyes, the room was empty. It had only been a dream. He hoped it was a sign.

With a sigh, Ryker dragged himself out of bed and brewed a strong pot of coffee. After showering and dressing, he finished his second cup of coffee. He had a short coughing fit on the strength of it and prepared to head to work. Staying home was his kryptonite.

Something had to give because Ryker didn't know how much longer he could go on without Oakley. Losing her would destroy the future they were meant to share, and the life they were just beginning to build. She was his heart, his home.

"Hey, Ryker," Jac called out, approaching Ryker as he entered Reynaud and Associates' building, his brow furrowed. "I spoke to Shandra again. She said there was another incident that she remembered. Evidently, the sister of a patient seemed agitated during their brother's last session. She can't identify her, but she hasn't left Oakley alone ever since."

"Oakley never mentioned it. Why didn't she mention it?" The anguish was loud in his voice.

and Audra's obsessive
thing happened in th
probably said too muc

"I appreciate all y
Charles lives now? Is I

"Oh, no. About si:
detained for his own ;
ly nice doctor, she's a
think."

"Addison? Doctor

"Yes, that sounds r
She got his social secur
I thought that was rea
not home, but I could

"So where is he?"

"Honestly? I don't
ed living home outside
that. I will tell you, tho
some medications, and
But that was before he 1
since."

"You've been so ve
information if needed?

"Sure. Let me give y
Jac took the numb
"Thank you again for ev

"I hope you find yo
were looking for."

"Doctor Oakley Ad
Her eyes grew large.

"It's her patient's confidentiality. You get it. Anyway, the sister had been calling and harassing her verbally during the workday, saying something about killing people's souls. Could be something, could be nothing. But I thought you should know."

Jac was back to using his guys, except for Alpha Team, to do their regular assignments. Garrett and Jac, and to some extent, Sharlee and Kaden, were always available if called into action, but the rest were working, checking in when jobs were completed. The girls had cooked so much food he had run out of freezer space and had asked them to stop. He wasn't interested in food eaten without Oakley.

"Thanks, Jac," Ryker responded, nodding appreciatively. "I assume you've already started following up on that lead. It might be our best shot right now."

"Right. If you want to go with one of the guys, you are welcome to do that. It looks like the brother lives or is staying in assisted living. I guess Oakley goes to see him at his facility."

"I'll go with the ones interviewing the friends and family. I am likely to strangle the brother if he gives me attitude."

"Good idea." Jac grabbed Ryker for a hug. Stepping back, he slapped Ryker on the back. "We are going to find her any moment. So when I say jump, you be ready."

"Love you, man."

"Back-atcha. Now let's stop this touchy-feely shit and find your girl."

Together, they spent hours interviewing the patient's friends and family, searching for any connection to Oakley's disappearance. But once again, they hit a wall. Then, when it was mentioned to

was nowhere to be f

"Now, don't qu

but Audra is not q

at least we know w

things to people, pl

ther hanging from

the military, well, I

people. I can't imag

"But Audra is obses

way, or she thinks y

opinion acceptable

group—something a

"What was their

"I have no idea,

about Charles. He w

decided to home-sch

sometimes he would

ing. Finally, she gave

doped him up. It did

ers to live around hin

"What happened

"I was gone for

here, Audra was back

been discharged fron

wear. She had some o

about then."

"What happened

"I don't know, rea

didn't return. The fan

"Thank you again."

Sharlee and Kaden worked on identifying the family members, finding them, and getting addresses. "I found where they lived. Not the people yet, but the sister should still live in the house, right? I'm checking utilities on the house. I sent the address to your cell phones. Garrett will meet you two there in twenty."

"Thanks, babe."

His gut jumped, and his heart rate rose. Would he say endearments to Oakley again? He stopped the thought.

"She could be there," said Ryker.

"Maybe, if Audra was so upset about it that she blamed Oakley, she might have done something like kidnap her," Jac said as they climbed into his SUV.

"Ryker, we'll find her," Jac reassured him, placing a hand on his shoulder. "It isn't a dead end. It's an elimination. We keep eliminating until we have only one viable option and close in. I do this every day. I know what I'm talking about, no matter how hard it is to wait. We won't stop until we find her safe and sound. "

But despite their best efforts, each hour seemed to bring more questions than answers. Ryker stopped in at work while waiting for more news. Doing his cases distracted him for a few minutes at a time, and he found comfort because he temporarily hired Shandra from Oakley's office as his personal assistant. It helped him feel as though his sweetling was just around the corner.

"I guess I can tell you now since I'm not working for her anymore."

"Tell me what? And don't forget that if Oakley wants you back, I won't be the competition."

"Oakley's last appointment on that Friday was with a new client named Amy Johnson," Shandra said. "It said prior client, but I couldn't find any record of an 'Amy Johnson' in our system. It's like that name appeared out of thin air."

Ryker's pulse quickened. A false identity? This was no coincidence. Someone had deliberately targeted Oakley.

Ryker picked up his phone and hit #2. Jac answered. "We need to find a woman called Amy Johnson," Ryker said, his jaw clenching. "She may be connected to Oakley's disappearance."

Jac agreed. "Sharlee can run a trace on the name and ID. If it's fake, we'll find out soon enough." He hesitated. "You know, some of Oakley's clients can be... unstable. Like Audra's brother Charles. It's possible one of them may have taken her."

Ryker swallowed hard, not wanting to consider that possibility. But he had to face the facts. As a psychiatrist, Oakley dealt with troubled people every day. Any of them could have a motive to hurt her.

"Where the hell is the police in all this?"

"Our contact is running the leads we find up the flagpole as we are. Sharing is caring, and the more we have on our side, the better."

"We should look into her recent cases as well," Ryker said. "No one is above suspicion right now."

Ryker prayed they found a lead that panned out soon. The longer Oakley remained missing, the greater the danger she was in. Ryker couldn't lose her now, not when they were so close to building a future together. He would do whatever it took to bring her home safely, even if it meant confronting dangerous suspects he would have normally left to the police.

Because a life without Oakley was no life at all.

"I need to get out. I'm coming your way," said Ryker.

"See you soon."

Oakley was his heart, his home, his entire world, and he would stop at nothing to save her. He would take her in any way she came so long as he could have her alive.

His thoughts shifted to Oakley's office manager. Shandra was efficient enough, but he remembered what Oakley had said about how she was not well-versed in office manager skills and confidentiality, so he wasn't impressed that she had waited until now to divulge important information. She said she was Oakley's friend, but he remembered Oakley didn't care for her work ethic, and they had never hung out since he'd known her. He would need to dissect that later.

He had an excellent office manager, so employing a personal assistant seemed appropriate because he was still positive that they would find Oakley. She would open her office back up and, if they both wanted to, hire Shandra back.

Yesterday, he finished another case and got an acceptable outcome. His clients were happy with him, but he didn't think he could do this forever. Loving Oakley and worrying about her had left him hypervigilant, grumpy, tired, desperate, and sad. Oakley would have enjoyed hearing about his last case. It had involved a first responder who was wrongfully accused of causing a death.

After connecting with Oakley, Ryker had refocused his life to choose her over work. He had discussed the legal status of her business and was amazed that she was the sole proprietor

"It's her patient's confidentiality. You get it. Anyway, the sister had been calling and harassing her verbally during the workday, saying something about killing people's souls. Could be something, could be nothing. But I thought you should know."

Jac was back to using his guys, except for Alpha Team, to do their regular assignments. Garrett and Jac, and to some extent, Sharlee and Kaden, were always available if called into action, but the rest were working, checking in when jobs were completed. The girls had cooked so much food he had run out of freezer space and had asked them to stop. He wasn't interested in food eaten without Oakley.

"Thanks, Jac," Ryker responded, nodding appreciatively. "I assume you've already started following up on that lead. It might be our best shot right now."

"Right. If you want to go with one of the guys, you are welcome to do that. It looks like the brother lives or is staying in assisted living. I guess Oakley goes to see him at his facility."

"I'll go with the ones interviewing the friends and family. I am likely to strangle the brother if he gives me attitude."

"Good idea." Jac grabbed Ryker for a hug. Stepping back, he slapped Ryker on the back. "We are going to find her any moment. So when I say jump, you be ready."

"Love you, man."

"Back-atcha. Now let's stop this touchy-feely shit and find your girl."

Together, they spent hours interviewing the patient's friends and family, searching for any connection to Oakley's disappearance. But once again, they hit a wall. Then, when it was mentioned to Charles' aunt that the sister, Audra Riley, was nowhere to be found, she said a strange thing.

"Now, don't quote me because I won't deal with the fallout, but Audra is not quite right. Well, neither of them were, but at least we know why Charles was off. Bi-polar does strange things to people, plus he hasn't been right since finding his father hanging from the stairwell handrail at seven. Then after the military, well, I'm sure you know what that does to some people. I can't imagine the horror." The woman shuddered. "But Audra is obsessive and controlling. She wants things her way, or she thinks you're against her. With that girl, the only opinion acceptable is hers. She's the leader of some odd group—something about medication misuse.

"What was their reason for forming?" asked Jac.

"I have no idea, really. But for Audra, it is probably all about Charles. He was kicked out of schools until his mother decided to home-school him, but that didn't work out because sometimes he would just sit in a room with the tv or radio blaring. Finally, she gave up, and when doctors couldn't help, they doped him up. It didn't help him, but it made it easier for others to live around him."

"What happened when he was grown?"

"I was gone for a while, but when I came back to live here, Audra was back in the home caring for Charles, who had been discharged from the military and looked worse for the wear. She had some of these medication veto people around her about then."

"What happened to their mother?"

"I don't know, really. My mom said she just left one day and didn't return. The family thinks that between Charles' crazies and Audra's obsessive control, it just ran her out. I heard something happened in the home, but honestly, I don't know. I've probably said too much."

"I appreciate all you've told me. Can you tell me where Charles lives now? Is he still with Audra?"

"Oh, no. About six months ago, he raged in public and was detained for his own and public safety. Then he found a really nice doctor, she's a psychiatrist, I think. Addi something, I think."

"Addison? Doctor Oakley Addison?"

"Yes, that sounds right. Anyway, it was upsetting to Audra. She got his social security and her income from caring for him. I thought that was really why she hated him being there and not home, but I could have misread things."

"So where is he?"

"Honestly? I don't know. I think he was moved to an assisted living home outside of the city. But I don't know more than that. I will tell you, though, now that he has a doctor and is on some medications, and he has friends, he looks so much better. But that was before he left for the new place. I haven't seen him since."

"You've been so very helpful. May I call you for clarifying information if needed?" asked Jac.

"Sure. Let me give you my number."

Jac took the number, and both men gave her their cards. "Thank you again for everything, Ma'am."

"I hope you find your friend. You didn't say who it was you were looking for."

"Doctor Oakley Addison."

Her eyes grew large. "Oh, I'm so sorry. I hope you find her."

"Thank you again."

Sharlee and Kaden worked on identifying the family members, finding them, and getting addresses. "I found where they lived. Not the people yet, but the sister should still live in the house, right? I'm checking utilities on the house. I sent the address to your cell phones. Garrett will meet you two there in twenty."

"Thanks, babe."

His gut jumped, and his heart rate rose. Would he say endearments to Oakley again? He stopped the thought.

"She could be there," said Ryker.

"Maybe, if Audra was so upset about it that she blamed Oakley, she might have done something like kidnap her," Jac said as they climbed into his SUV.

"Ryker, we'll find her," Jac reassured him, placing a hand on his shoulder. "It isn't a dead end. It's an elimination. We keep eliminating until we have only one viable option and close in. I do this every day. I know what I'm talking about, no matter how hard it is to wait. We won't stop until we find her safe and sound. "

But despite their best efforts, each hour seemed to bring more questions than answers. Ryker stopped in at work while waiting for more news. Doing his cases distracted him for a few minutes at a time, and he found comfort because he temporarily hired Shandra from Oakley's office as his personal assistant. It helped him feel as though his sweetling was just around the corner.

"I guess I can tell you now since I'm not working for her anymore."

"Tell me what? And don't forget that if Oakley wants you back, I won't be the competition."

"Oakley's last appointment on that Friday was with a new client named Amy Johnson," Shandra said. "It said prior client, but I couldn't find any record of an 'Amy Johnson' in our system. It's like that name appeared out of thin air."

Ryker's pulse quickened. A false identity? This was no coincidence. Someone had deliberately targeted Oakley.

Ryker picked up his phone and hit #2. Jac answered. "We need to find a woman called Amy Johnson," Ryker said, his jaw clenching. "She may be connected to Oakley's disappearance."

Jac agreed. "Sharlee can run a trace on the name and ID. If it's fake, we'll find out soon enough." He hesitated. "You know, some of Oakley's clients can be... unstable. Like Audra's brother Charles. It's possible one of them may have taken her."

Ryker swallowed hard, not wanting to consider that possibility. But he had to face the facts. As a psychiatrist, Oakley dealt with troubled people every day. Any of them could have a motive to hurt her.

"Where the hell is the police in all this?"

"Our contact is running the leads we find up the flagpole as we are. Sharing is caring, and the more we have on our side, the better."

"We should look into her recent cases as well," Ryker said. "No one is above suspicion right now."

Ryker prayed they found a lead that panned out soon. The longer Oakley remained missing, the greater the danger she was in. Ryker couldn't lose her now, not when they were so close to building a future together. He would do whatever it took to bring her home safely, even if it meant confronting dangerous suspects he would have normally left to the police.

Because a life without Oakley was no life at all.

"I need to get out. I'm coming your way," said Ryker.

"See you soon."

Oakley was his heart, his home, his entire world, and he would stop at nothing to save her. He would take her in any way she came so long as he could have her alive.

His thoughts shifted to Oakley's office manager. Shandra was efficient enough, but he remembered what Oakley had said about how she was not well-versed in office manager skills and confidentiality, so he wasn't impressed that she had waited until now to divulge important information. She said she was Oakley's friend, but he remembered Oakley didn't care for her work ethic, and they had never hung out since he'd known her. He would need to dissect that later.

He had an excellent office manager, so employing a personal assistant seemed appropriate because he was still positive that they would find Oakley. She would open her office back up and, if they both wanted to, hire Shandra back.

Yesterday, he finished another case and got an acceptable outcome. His clients were happy with him, but he didn't think he could do this forever. Loving Oakley and worrying about her had left him hypervigilant, grumpy, tired, desperate, and sad. Oakley would have enjoyed hearing about his last case. It had involved a first responder who was wrongfully accused of causing a death.

After connecting with Oakley, Ryker had refocused his life to choose her over work. He had discussed the legal status of her business and was amazed that she was the sole proprietor but had very little other than an LLC set up. He'd quickly brought Oakley in as a client and settled her business affairs. Just a week after she'd returned to town, she'd asked him if he would be her second on the business. Not partnership, but as her attorney. Did she have a premonition?

"Ryker," Sharlee's voice cut through his thoughts when he arrived. "We found something. You need to see this."

"Lead the way," he said, determination flaring within him. He seemed to be living at either Jac's office or IT when he wasn't in his own office. He slept wherever he landed.

Ryker stood in Sharlee's IT department office, tugging at the knot of his tie, feeling the tightness of it closing around his throat. Jac and Garrett appeared in the large room filled with electronics. Ryker clenched his jaw, and the vein throbbed beneath the closely cropped beard that he had recently begun to grow. It was rebellious, but it said he still controlled some things.

Charlotte waved the men out of her room, directing them to the conference room.

Garrett looked around. "I guess we better hit the conference room. Charlotte gets upset when we get too close to her metal boxes."

Sharlee agreed. "I don't like extra heat in here. It could melt my precious equipment."

Garrett laughed. "I figured you had a reason besides being bossy and territorial."

She grunted in a close imitation of her husband's sound of disgruntled agreement.

As they strode down the hallway, Jac's people started toward the conference room. The long table was filling with their former military cohorts, and current Alpha members–Jac, Sharlee, Levi, Monroe, Carter, Callie, Garrett, Mark, and Kaden were all there. Each an expert in their respective fields, they were all prepared to go as far as they needed to; laws weren't boundaries when family was at stake. They would save Oakley. Ryker sat next to Monroe and jiggled his leg in anxious anticipation.

"Alright, team," said Jac, tapping his foot impatiently. "Let's get to work. Charlotte, I need you to share the information you have about Oakley's last known interactions and her clients."

"Got it," Sharlee responded, her fingers tapping furiously on her keyboard. Her green eyes locked onto the screen, the furrow in her brow deepening as she delved into the digital world in a new direction.

"Levi, Kaden, I want you two to follow any leads that come up. Carter, Mark, you're on your own jobs but keep in touch. Callie, when Sharlee gets the number, and you are tied in, I want you to monitor the phone lines of this Audra or Amy or whoever we find. Monroe, we'll need your expertise in strategizing as we get more info, so continue running the ops scenarios while we wait," Jac instructed, his voice steady and commanding. "Garrett, you have the ops until we need you.

Meanwhile, Mark approached the video screen that Jessie, Ivy, and Mallory had appeared on, his expression serious. "Ladies, I need you all to be extra careful right now. No one goes out alone, and if you can avoid going out at all, even better. Work from home until we find Oakley."

The women exchanged glances, clearly unhappy with the restrictions. Jessie spoke up first, her voice tinged with frustration. "We've been through this before, Mark. We know how to handle ourselves. Besides, I've been cleared to return to work. I was going to bring Anora with me. We discussed this."

"Of course you do," he replied softly, his eyes filled with concern. Jessie and his newborn had changed the hard, dark Mark to someone who smiled at his wife and cajoled instead of demanded. "But we can't afford to take any chances right now. We must focus on finding Oakley and ensuring everyone stays safe."

In the conference room, Callie folded her arms across her chest, her blue eyes narrowing. "I'm part of this team and intend to be out there helping."

"Callie, we know you're more than capable," Garrett interjected, placing a reassuring hand on her shoulder. "But right now, we need you in the supportive, onsite role. It's just as important as being in the field."

She sighed but nodded reluctantly, understanding the importance of her role and her man's need to keep her safe.

"Becky," said Carter, "You have to stay in the office, like Callie, and lunch will be delivered, or you need to bring your own. I'll drop you off and bring you home, or you will go with Jac and Sharlee if I'm out."

Becky sighed, screwed up her face but nodded. As the women agreed to the restrictions, they turned their attention back to the mission at hand, knowing that the sooner they found Oakley, the sooner they could return to normalcy.

Ryker surveyed the room, his heart swelling with gratitude for the unwavering support of his friends and teammates. Together, they would find Oakley and bring her home–and they would do it without leaving anyone behind.

Jac turned to Ryker. "I'm putting Mark in charge of the tactical. You're support."

"Jac, I don't mind running the leads and all the support you need, but I have to be there when we find Oakley."

"Fine, but until then, you're with Carter or one of the guys."

"I can live with that."

"Good," said Jac, "Because I wasn't asking."

"Guys," Sharlee announced, her voice laced with urgency. "I found something."

All eyes turned to her as she pulled up a file on her laptop. "Oakley was working with a patient who has PTSD and bipolar disorder. His sister blames Oakley for his condition."

"I believe we know who that is but is that her real name?" Ryker asked, leaning over Sharlee's shoulder to get a better look at the screen.

"Her name is Audra," Sharlee replied, scrolling through the information she had found. "She cared for her brother for years, ever since their mother left after their father died. She was completely dependent on him emotionally and financially. They were inseparable."

"Audra's life wasn't easy," Sharlee continued, her brow furrowing in concentration. "She had a failed marriage before her brother's diagnosis. Her husband was abusive, and her brother saved her from that nightmare. "

"I guess moral obligations mean nothing," grumbled Mallory.

"Saved her?" Jac inquired, his face etched with worry.

"Apparently, he intervened between his sister and her abusive spouse during a particularly violent episode. Audra left her husband for good after that," Sharlee explained. "Her brother became her rock, of sorts, even though he was currently being medically discharged. He was ultimately diagnosed as suffering from PTSD and Bipolar."

Kaden continued. "He was discharged from the Army, but not medically at first. Later it looks like a traumatic experience during deployment led to his PTSD, which came nearly four years after his second hitch. He took the natural out after eight years, right before his sister moved in with him and their mother. For the last six years, it looks like she's devoted much of her adult life to caring for him. Their mother left right after Audra's failed marriage. Evidently, they couldn't get services, and he tried to kill his mother in a PTSD episode during a manic phase."

Garrett sucked in a hard breath. "Fuck, that man went through hell, and the military missed the diagnosis?"

"I don't know if he told them. He just didn't reenlist," said Kaden.

Sharlee continued. "His mother likely left because it was dangerous. That is probably why she left him, he was an adult, so with no legal obligation and no services, she just didn't know what to do. Our Oakley diagnosed his Bipolar and, ultimately, PTSD. She got his disability with the military, and social security qualified him for disability due to Bipolar, but it took him going to a facility to get it all finalized."

"Oakley likely saved this man's future happiness. It sounds like the siblings have a strong bond," Callie remarked, her arms folded across her chest.

"Too strong," Sharlee muttered, her eyes narrowing as she delved deeper into Audra's backstory. "Her co-dependency on her brother became unhealthy. When Oakley began treating him, Audra saw it as a threat. Audra believes Oakley took her brother away from her. It's in Oakley's notes."

"Enough to kidnap her?" Ryker asked, his jaw clenching as he considered the implications.

"Maybe," Sharlee replied, her voice filled with determination. "But we need more information. We need to find out if Audra had any contact with Oakley before she disappeared."

"Let's get on it," Jac said, his tone firm and resolute. "We need to find Oakley, and if this is our best lead, we're going after it."

"Where can we find the brother?" asked Monroe. "He is our best lead."

As the team began investigating Audra and her involvement in Oakley's disappearance, they knew they were entering dangerous territory. But with each new piece of information, they grew more determined to bring Oakley home–and to make those responsible pay for their actions. And they believed it very likely was Audra.

Kaden threw a picture of an assisted living place and an address on the overhead monitor. "I found him."

Carter stood and leaned over to kiss Becky. "I'm going. If I'm not back before Jac and Sharlee go home, you know what to do."

Becky rolled her eyes, and Carter leaned close to whisper something in her ear. Becky blushed and nodded. Carter nodded back and dropped another heated kiss on her forehead.

Mark grabbed his gear and headed out with Carter. "Stay home, Jessica," he yelled at the screen with her face on it.

The video call ended, and all the women's faces vanished.

Things were hopping, and Ryker couldn't help but feed on the energy. He had to believe they would find her very soon.

Chapter 9

Carter and Mark stood in the reception area of the Fire Mountain Manor, an assisted living facility for those struggling with medication management and community living.

"May I help you?"

"Yes, we are here to visit Charles Greely."

"I'll have to ask if he wants a visit. May I have your name?"

Mark pulled out his card that identified him as securities and a prior Marine. Carter's showed securities and prior Army. The woman gave them a long look. Both men knew when they were being sized up for someone's night of fantasy as she finally drew her eyes away, saying she'd be back as she walked down the hall.

When the receptionist returned, she brought a fit man with her. It was obvious he had been a bigger man before, but he still held many attributes of someone who took pride in who he was. He approached and put out his hand.

"Gentlemen, what can I do for you?"

"Charles Greely?" asked Mark.

"Yes, would you like to take a seat?"

The men nodded. Carter began. "Thank you for talking to us. We are working on a missing persons case and believe you might help us?"

"Okay, why?"

"Do you have a sister?"

"Audra. Yes. Is she okay?" Charles' demeanor stiffened in concern.

"As far as we know, yes. But we don't have that information because we are trying to find her to speak to her. We just don't know where she lives. We hoped," Mark spoke collaboratively, "that you might have an idea."

"This missing person isn't Audra, right?"

"No, we should have been clearer," said Carter. "We understand you both know the woman. She's a psychiatrist, Oakley Addison."

"Dr. Addison is missing?"

"She has been for over two weeks. We understand the last person she saw in her office was your sister, Audra. We want to ask her about the state of Dr. Addison on that visit."

"Are you sure? I mean, Audra didn't like Dr. Addison."

Mark pulled out his phone and showed a photo of the woman on the video camera in the waiting room. "Is this your sister?"

Charles leaned over and grabbed the cell phone. "Damn, it is her."

Mark continued. "Do you have any idea why she made the appointment under the name of 'Amy Johnson.'"

"My mother's middle name and her maiden name. Audra blames Dr. Addison for my being hospitalized and then choosing to stay here for a while to stabilize. She's wrong about this being a harmful place because the hospital and now here are the best choices I have made since getting the diagnosis. I'll leave here in a few months, but until then, I am building my confidence and can live a much better life. This is all due to Dr. Addison's help."

"But your sister didn't see it that way?" asked Mark.

"No. She wanted me to stay with her, waste my life doing nothing of value. She's depressed and angry since her divorce. She quit her job and helped me until Dr. Addison made these arrangements. I'm not going back to stay with Audra when I get out. I'm going to get my own place and a job. My hope is I can convince her to do the same, but I'm not sure that's possible. But I intend to try." Charles' voice was firm and determined.

"I hope that works out for both of you," said Carter. "Can you tell us where she lives now because we have checked the home you both lived in, and it was not being occupied at present."

"She's not there? I knew she was acting very strange the last time she came by, and that's been about two weeks or so. I can't quite remember... oh shit. She usually comes at least twice a week." He shook his head and gave them a worried look that the men didn't like. "Dr. Addison stopped checking on me a little over two weeks ago. I'm positive it's been a while. How could I have not noticed?" He placed his head on his open palms. "Audra, what have you done?" He looked at the men. "The only thing we have is my father's old fishing cabin out in the woods, but it's pretty run down. I don't think she would stay out there."

"Is there an address?" asked Carter.

Charles gave them a grim smile. "Nope, but I can draw you a map."

GARRETT, RYKER, MONROE, and Jac stood behind Kaden, squinting at the grainy security camera footage from a convenience store near Oakley's workplace. In the footage, a man in a hooded sweatshirt lingered in the shadows, his face obscured but his posture unmistakably predatory.

"Could he be our guy?" Ryker asked, studying the screen intently.

"Can't say for sure, but it's the closest thing we've got to a lead right now," Sharlee replied, her eyes narrowed in concentration. "See him get in that SUV. Kinda looks like the one described by the security guard, George."

"I hate that we had finally gotten into the video cams at the garage, and they were corrupted. They say it has happened before. I say they need better safeguards in place. Some things were great; some, like viruses, are unacceptable."

"I'll get on that right after we find Oakley. Meanwhile, we need to dig deeper. We can't afford to overlook anything," Ryker said, his resolve unwavering.

Jac's phone rang. "Mark, what do you have?"

Jac listened for a little bit and nodded. "No, come back. We need to regroup." Jac turned to the others. "Mark and Carter might have something." He proceeded to give them the little he had. The men would share the rest when they arrived.

Ryker needed to stay alert and focused, though exhaustion threatened to overtake him. In the two weeks since Oakley's disappearance, he'd hardly slept or eaten, devoting every waking moment to the search and doing what he could to help.

But so far, they'd had few leads. The imposter client remained a strong focus, but they needed to find Audra. Several were headed up to the cabin today. Other than the last client, none of Oakley's recent cases seemed suspicious, so this was all they had to go on. Ryker had interviewed Shandra and her office neighbors multiple times, and their stories matched as best as possible. What he wanted to do was find Bella, but like Oakley, no one had seen or heard from Bella since she left work that Friday evening. There were only two likely scenarios: she was part of the reason Oakley was missing, or she was taken as well.

Bella seemed to genuinely care for Oakley whenever she talked to her. She'd questioned Ryker's motivations, and he had respected that. He had said nothing, although he didn't fully trust her motivations. He sensed that she was attracted to him and worried she might try to take advantage of the times earlier situations had left him and Bella alone. He was suspicious of everyone and everything. He didn't have any concrete evidence to suggest she was involved. He decided to stay cautious for now.

Running a hand through his hair, Ryker fought back his frustration. Yes, they might find Audra, but then what. Would she have Oakley, or if she knew where she was, would she tell them? If she didn't know or didn't tell, they would be no closer to finding Oakley, and time was running out. If they didn't uncover a solid lead soon, the likelihood of rescuing her alive decreased with each passing day.

He couldn't give up hope. Ryker replayed every detail of their investigation, searching for something he may have missed. There had to be a clue, a thread they could pull to unravel the mystery of Oakley's disappearance. He just had to find it.

The team gathered in the dimly lit conference room, tension and anxiety radiating from each. Ryker clenched his jaw as he stared at the screen displaying a grainy image of Audra, captured by one of their informants.

"Alright, listen up," Sharlee began, her voice cutting through the silence. "Our informant managed to get us solid intel on Audra's involvement in Oakley's disappearance. It appears she's holding her captive at one of the properties owned by either her or the group she is involved with."

Ryker's heart raced, fury bubbling beneath the surface. "How can we be sure this is accurate?" he demanded, his voice strained.

"Because our informant is someone close to Audra, someone who's been monitoring her movements. Someone who fears discovery but fears more how erratic Audra has become." Sharlee replied, her blue eyes locking onto his. "We're not taking any chances here."

"Charlotte," Jac continued, turning to the Vaper of the Internet, "you've got contacts in the dark. Reach out and see if anyone's noticed anything suspicious near these properties. We need all the intel we can get."

"Already in the works."

The team huddled around the huge computer monitors, eyes flicking between Sharlee and the screen as she typed furiously. Her fingers flew across the keyboard, using her extensive knowledge of hacking to break into the city's real estate database.

"Got it," Sharlee announced, exhaling heavily. On the screen, several properties Audra and her group owned were displayed. "Now we just need to narrow it down."

"Let's start with the most likely locations based on their recent activities," Callie suggested, her analytical mind working in overdrive.

"Sharlee," said Mark, "start researching the security measures and access points for each property. We need to be prepared for whatever we face."

"What about the cabin?"

"Yes, the cabin is either a red herring or the perfect location. We will check all three out."

"Looks like we've got our targets," Jac declared, studying the satellite images of the three sites. "But we need to be careful. These places are bound to have security measures in place if they are using them."

"Agreed," Levi nodded. "We'll need to find a way to bypass any alarms and cameras before we get inside for a look. Sharlee?"

"Leave that to me," Sharlee chimed in confidently. "I'm setting up the hack into their systems, and each building has them. I'm disabling everything remotely. But be cautious anyway."

"Good," Ryker said, clenching his jaw. "We can't risk alerting them to our presence. We don't know what they might do to Oakley if they realize we're coming."

"Then what's the plan?" Callie asked, her voice low and focused.

"Alright, here's what we know," Mark said, stepping forward. "There are three properties that could potentially be where Oakley is being held - a secluded cabin owned by her and her brother, a warehouse, or an abandoned building in the city, both owned by members of the group. We'll need to split up and investigate each location simultaneously."

"Callie and I will take the warehouse," Garrett announced, determination etched across his face. "I'll grab a few loose cannons from Bravo Team.

"I'll cover the cabin," Mark said, his voice steady and resolute. "Ryker, you're with me. Somehow I think it has more potential."

"Then I'll take the abandoned building," said Carter. "I'll grab Levi and one or two guys from the assignment board.

The act of actually moving on intel about where Oakley was likely to be nearly was his mental undoing. "Garrett, when do we go?" Ryker asked, his pulse pounding in his ears. The thought of Oakley being held against her will, scared and out of her mind, fueled him with a desperate urgency.

"Jac, you with me?" asked Mark. Typically, Jac stayed with Monroe to strategize or worked with Sharlee when the job required. Only for personal or high stakes did he enter the fray himself.

"You read my mind." Jac wouldn't allow Ryker to go with Mark without a buffer. He was the best buffer in this case. He knew the stakes were high, but for Ryker, there didn't seem to be a boundary left that would stop him from rushing into the situation like a roaring lion seeking to avenge. Jac would have to be that barrier both emotionally and physically.

"Remember, we don't know what kind of security measures they have in place, so be prepared for anything," Sharlee warned. "I'm trying to do my best to locate anything, but so far, I'm coming up empty. It doesn't seem quite right."

"Alright, let's cut the chatter and gear up," Mark commanded. "Kaden, work with Monroe. Can we get a drone in the air?"

"We can, but unfortunately, I can only go to one spot, so pick your best guess, and I'll go set up with that team."

This was personal, and Ryker had suddenly become, in his own mind, mission essential. He had trained with Jac for exercise and male bonding after the military, occasionally even running simulated missions for grins and giggles, but now that it counted, he was glad he had.

As the team finalized their rescue plans, Callie approached them with a grim expression. "I just intercepted some communications from the informant to another member. Oakley's being drugged - they're giving her something to make her hallucinate and lose touch with reality."

"What the fuck!" Ryker clenched his fists in frustration; desperation, anger, and fear jockeyed for primary emotional position... his gut continually churning and boiling. Sharlee furrowed her brow, her blue eyes filled with concern.

"Did you find out what exactly they're giving her?" Mark asked, his voice tense.

"Looks like a blend of powerful antipsychotics and hallucinogens," Callie replied, the disgust evident in her voice. "It's designed to break her mentally so she can't fight back or escape. And to make a point. Psychiatric medication is deadly."

"Jesus," Mallory muttered under her breath, horrified at the thought of what Oakley must be going through.

Ryker's heart raced at the urgency of the situation, and he could barely contain his rage. "We need to get her out of there as soon as possible, before the effects become irreversible."

"Agreed," Mark said solemnly. "Let's move out. Let's find her."

Jac reiterated the mission. "We get in, we locate the most likely place for Oakley, and we get out. Then we regroup and go in strong."

With a renewed sense of urgency, the team advanced towards the building, ready to face whatever challenges lay ahead in order to save Oakley from her torment.

"Let's move out. The sooner we're in, the sooner we're out with the answers and ready to return to finish the job." Mark urged, as the team gathered their gear and headed towards their designated raid building. "Sharlee will be the voice of Go because hers is distinctive, and she knows when the security and cameras are disabled. When you hear her, that is your activation but no heroics. This is a recon mission only. When we enter for real, we go in with a full complement of operatives. Let's get this done so we can get Oakley and us home safe and sound. Get in, get out, regroup for the final rescue."

Sharlee added. "Since you are going in simultaneously, I will disengage the buildings' surveillance and alarm systems before giving the go. Can't have any screw-ups."

As each micro-team approached their respective building, each determined to find Audra's hiding spot. The adrenaline was running so high that it took sheer willpower to not go rampaging through the building looking for whom they sought.

Sharlee gave the signal to advance, and just like finely tuned race cars, the men advanced on their site with stealth and tightly wound energy. The cabin was the smallest and easiest to breach. While it appeared someone had been there recently, if Oakley had been there, she no longer was. The three quickly cleared the surrounding area and reported their findings before retreating to their SUV and returning to Sharlee and the command center.

The next group to report in was at the abandoned building. "Fuck, this place is huge, but luckily, we have Kaden, and except for a couple of bums squatting in the place, it's empty. We checked the rooms to make sure."

The final building, the warehouse, seemed abandoned at first. They could see that a chain-link fence surrounded it topped with barbed wire. The terrain around the building was uneven and littered with debris–a challenging landscape to navigate without being seen or heard.

As the team drew closer, it was obvious that someone or ones occupied it, but until they made their way inside, there wasn't going to be much verification. The grounds were littered with junk, and while it could provide cover, it also made it difficult to navigate.

Finally, they could position themselves close enough to get a clear view through some of the newly replaced windowpanes. There was an area of windows in the back corner of the building that was blocked with bits of wood from the inside. Odd because the glass was still intact.

"That's where she is. Bet you a dozen donuts," said Callie into her com. Garrett smiled. His girl could eat a dozen in one sitting.

"You're on, Callie Girl."

The group of four operatives did a recon of the area and the building from the exterior. Then they took count of the inhabitants the best they could, realizing it was daylight. When it was evening, those numbers would likely dwindle greatly.

"Alright, we have our intel. Let's move out," ordered Garrett. As he got into the SUV to drive off, he said, "Fuck, I'm too old for this."

Callie laughed along with the two other operatives. "Can I quote you on that, dear?"

"Not if you know what's good for you, sweetheart." The group laughed louder.

JAC STOOD AT THE HEAD of the table in their conference room, scanning the faces of his assembled team. They had borrowed a few more to round out the rescue team to fourteen. More, and it would be hard to get in unnoticed. They had located Audra's hideout two hours ago, and now it was time to execute their plan to rescue Oakley.

It would be dark in another hour, and they would be ready. The air was thick with anticipation, and Ryker clenched his jaw, then took a deep breath, fully aware of the weight resting on everyone's shoulders. Sharlee cued up an audio clip on the main overhead monitor.

The room fell silent as Sharlee, the unsurpassed deep diver of the worldwide dark web and more, played the audio recording intercepted just hours ago. Ryker's jaw clenched as he listened to Audra's voice, cold and calculating, discussing her plans for Oakley.

"Got this from a wiretap we'd set up on one of Audra's known associates," Sharlee explained once the recording ended. "She slipped up and mentioned keeping Oakley in the warehouse owned by the group. So, we are right on the money."

"She sounds like she's lost her grip on reality. It's fanaticism and more," observed Monroe.

Ryker's eyes narrowed. His anger was palpable. "We need to find her now. I can't even imagine what she's going through."

"Mark, let's go over the entry plan," Garrett continued, gesturing for the rugged man to join him at the head of the table. "We'll need to be swift and silent, assuming there might be guards or security measures in place that are not electronic."

"Affirmative," Mark replied, his deep-set eyes focused on the task. "I've got a few ideas for breaching the property without raising alarms that Monroe and I have gone over. We can use suppressed weapons, night vision goggles, and other tactical gear to ensure we stay under the radar for as long as possible."

Ryker nodded, his mind racing with thoughts of what Oakley must be enduring at that very moment. He knew they couldn't afford any mistakes, not with her life on the line.

"Once inside," Mark continued, "hopefully Kaden will have heat signatures, and we can identify not only trouble, but where they are keeping her. Unfortunately, we must go on an educated guess because the heat signatures don't come with names attached. Even though we believe we know where they are keeping Oakley, and Carter and Ryker will go in there first, we'll search room by room. Maintain continuous radio contact with our command center. If we encounter resistance, we neutralize it as quickly and quietly as possible. Our primary objective is to find Oakley and get her out safely. Everything else is secondary."

"Understood," Carter confirmed, his military training kicking into high gear.

"Okay, listen up," Mark said, his voice serious and authoritative, cutting through the tense atmosphere. "We've got one shot at this, so we need to ensure we're prepared for anything. Once we arrive at the property, we'll split into three teams—one for entry and scrubbing, one for extraction, and one for backup and rear clean up. Levi and Jac, you'll lead the entry team with me. Carter and Ryker, you are recovery. Jac, you will slide into extraction if it looks like you need to. Otherwise, work with backup. Bravo, you are rear entrance. Since you know each other, you will be better off working together.

"Ryker, you are with Carter until we clear the building; then, you are solely on Oakley duty. We don't know what state she will be in, so having you talk to her will make the difference between a quick exit or a messy one. Once she is out, you and Carter get her to the hospital."

"That leaves me and Callie to work the backup," said Garrett. "We got that covered."

Callie nodded. "We'll watch your six, so you can get to Oakley."

"Kaden and Sharlee, you two will be on surveillance. Monroe, you are our strategist. We need eyes on the ground, watching for any movement or signs of trouble and a way to circumvent that trouble if possible."

"Roger that," said Monroe. Kaden and Sharlee nodded in unison.

"Yes! I'll finally get to use my tricked-out vehicle on a mission." Jac looked at his too-excited wife and issued his warning.

"If you get out of the vehicle during the execution of this recovery, you won't be sitting comfortably for quite a while. Get me?"

Sharlee couldn't suppress her grin. She gave him a civilian's version of a salute. "Aye, aye, Captain. Support only."

Most in the room knew Jac was remembering when Sharlee went off on her own and showed up at a live situation in her new SUV, hoping to monitor and do her job from the scene. That didn't go so well, but it was a turning point in their relationship.

"Charlotte," came Jac's warning reply.

"Understood," Sharlee responded, her fingers already flying across the keyboard of her laptop, setting up the necessary surveillance equipment to be engaged in the SUV.

"Before we leave, let's go over the gear we'll need," Carter said, moving towards a table laden with various supplies. "Night-vision goggles, body armor, lock-picking kits, and lasers. We want to keep things as quiet as possible, so no guns unless absolutely necessary. We have our standard issue if we need them."

As the team members gathered their equipment, Ryker could feel the tension in the room. Each person knew the stakes of this mission, and the potential consequences if they failed. Mark, who was in charge of this mission, turned to face them, his expression serious.

"Listen up," he said, his voice firm. "I know we're all worried about Oakley, but we need to stay focused. She's being forcibly given medication that's causing her to experience psychosis and hallucinations. She will be unpredictable."

Ryker added, "And if we don't get her out of there soon, her condition could worsen–" his voice caught for a moment, "–or even become fatal."

Jac spoke. The gravity of the situation evident in his eyes. "And if we don't do this right, Oakley could be further harmed, and Audra might escape. I'm not losing operatives on this because we were ill-prepared. Study the schematics, familiarize yourself with where the van will be, our vehicles, and escapes, you know the drill. Success is the only acceptable outcome."

"Remember," Jac continued, connecting with each team member's gaze, "we're Oakley's lifeline. She's depending on us. We can't afford any mistakes."

The room was filled with silent nods as they absorbed his words. Mark took one last look at the assembled group, their faces filled with determination and resolve. With a nod, he signaled that it was time to move out.

Chapter 10

A rriving at the fenced area, they waited for Sharlee to give them the go-ahead.

"Stay low and keep to the shadows," Mark instructed, leading the march as they carefully picked their way through the obstacles. "The last thing we want is for them to see us coming."

"Once we're inside," Callie whispered, "we have to make sure Oakley stays protected. She might not even understand what's happening, and she could panic or try to escape."

"Understood," Ryker replied, his ever-present determination burning bright within him. They were so close to rescuing Oakley, and nothing would stand in their way. Bravo team split off to find the back exit.

The operatives divided into their teams and took the entrances assigned to them. There were three main entrances, and with the added men, they could cover all easily.

"Let's do this," said Levi. Those around him nodded their agreement. The drone went up, so they knew the security for the building was neutralized.

"Heat signatures are eight. One is separated off to the far eastern corner of the building. Not moving. Supine. Best guess, it's Oakley."

"One guard by the entrance," Mark whispered into his headset, his voice barely audible as the team huddled together behind a row of bushes. "Armed with a semi-automatic."

"Same at the back," confirmed Garrett.

"Any other points of entry?" Levi asked, scanning the perimeter for alternative options.

Sharlee's voice rang clear in the earpieces. "Go! Go! Go!

The night was overcast, a thick blanket of clouds obscuring the moon as Ryker and the team neared Audra's hideout. The darkness enveloped their approach, providing some cover as they crept forward with cautious determination. Ryker clenched his jaw in anticipation, his heart pounding like a relentless drum in his chest.

Then, as they began to peel the layers of debris and old equipment, they heard a sound, then more. Then, just before they approached the door at the end of the building, it opened on them. Without thought, they dove around the corner, with Mark maintaining his position behind the door. When it began to close, Levi and Mark neutralized the two men and stashed them at the backside of the building.

The front group took point while Carter and Ryker had one mission only, locate Oakley, recover, and get the hell out of Dodge.

The back four from Bravo team verified they were in position.

"I'm coming, sweetling," Ryker whispered. Then he cleared his mind and put one focus in place. Retrieve and retreat.

"Only one other door, on the eastern side," Callie reported, her eyes flicking to her smartphone as she assessed the building's layout, sent by Kaden. "But it's likely to be locked or alarmed."

"Not alarmed. That's been taken care of."

"Alright," Carter said, his voice low and steady. "Ryker, you're with me. We'll try the east door because it's the closest, while Mark and Jac create a diversion at the front. Sharlee will keep her ears open, and Kaden, keep your eyes peeled."

"Roger. I've got you covered. This drone is silent."

As Mark and Jac slipped away to execute the diversion, Ryker and Carter made their way toward the eastern side of the building. Bravo were in their assigned positions. The carpet remnants from bygone days of management offices muffled their footsteps, careful not to make a sound. As the group neared the door, Ryker felt an icy chill of dread creeping up his spine, but he pushed it aside, focusing on the task at hand.

"Locked, just as we thought," Carter murmured, examining the heavy steel door. "But I can bypass this lock. Just give me a minute." He pulled out his tools.

Ryker nodded, his breath hitching as he heard the faint sounds of gunfire and shouting from the front of the property. The diversion was underway. He prayed that the team would remain unharmed while they drew the guards away from their true point of entry.

Carter expertly picked the lock, and the door creaked open just a crack, revealing the dimly lit interior of the hideout.

"Got it," Carter whispered triumphantly as the soft beep of the disarmed alarm system filled the air. All systems were a go. Ryker tried not to focus on what was going on up front and the safety of his friends. Oakley was his mission.

Ryker's hand instinctively reached for the pistol holstered at his side.

Carter whispered. "Stay close and stay alert. We don't know who or what we might encounter in here."

Together, they stepped into the ominous darkness, their senses on high alert, searching for any sign of Oakley or Audra's associates. Their goggles were doing what they were meant to do. Allow them to see. Each step they took felt like a gamble, the risk of being caught looming over them like a suffocating shroud, but the nightshades helped. The ominous atmosphere in this area was oppressing, and the thought of Oakley in this for weeks propelled him to enter deeper into the evil web of despair.

"Remember," Ryker thought, his heart racing with anxiety and adrenaline, "we're doing this for Oakley. Failure is not an option."

Ryker's heart pounded like a drum in his chest. He scanned the narrow hallways, alert for any signs of danger or the faintest hint of Oakley's presence. Carter was one step ahead of Ryker, and the tension was rolling off him in what seemed like visual waves.

As they rounded a corner, the men caught sight of a door left slightly ajar. With a quick signal, Carter cautiously approached the door, his hand gripping his gun tightly. They were going to go as quietly as possible, but with the skirmish dying down in the front, they had to move quickly.

"Oakley," Ryker breathed as Carter pushed the door open and revealed a dimly lit room where Oakley was slumped against the wall, her eyes unfocused and glassy.

"Fuck! Oakley!" Ryker said in a stage whisper as he rushed forward, his heart twisting painfully as he took in her disheveled appearance. Her once vibrant eyes now looked wild and unrecognizable. "Baby, it's me, Ryker. We're here to get you out."

"Ryker?" Oakley murmured, her voice shaking. "No, no... You can't be real. You're just another hallucination. Go away!"

Carter watched the door with Callie and now Garrett, covering the two inside.

"Oakley, listen to me." Ryker knelt beside her, gently grabbing her face between his hands. "Remember that night we went stargazing on the roof of my parent's summer home? I told you about my favorite constellation, Orion, and how my dad used to take me camping to watch the stars. Only you would know that."

Her eyes widened in recognition, and a tear rolled down her cheek as she whispered his name. "Ryker"

"Let's get her out of here," said Carter. "We need to hurry before more guards show up." He tapped his ear come. "We're coming your way, Sharlee. Kaden, what is our best way out?"

"The way you came in. But hurry."

With Ryker supporting Oakley, the team retraced their steps, their senses heightened as they navigated through the warehouse's labyrinthine corridors. The sound of footsteps echoed behind them, and Nathan, one of their extras, took a position at a corner, firing warning shots to deter any pursuers.

"Almost there," Carter reassured, his eyes darting around for any potential threats.

As they emerged from the hideout into the night air, it was clear that the mission had taken its toll on each member of the team. Mark sported a bruised jaw, while Jac's knuckles were bloodied from an altercation. Levi was a little bloody, but Garrett looked like he and Callie had just gone on a date. Callie looked a little more worn out. Despite their injuries, they wore expressions of relief, knowing they had saved Oakley from a terrible fate.

"Where's Audra?" Sharlee asked.

Ryker watched as several scanned the surroundings for any sign of the woman responsible for Oakley's suffering.

"Dammit! She must have escaped during the chaos," Ryker muttered, frustration bubbling beneath his exhaustion as he cradled Oakley close.

"Oh, she did. I saw her booking it out a far door we didn't see before, but we were all occupied, so she got away." Callie grimaced. Garrett grinned, holding up a backpack. "Yeah, well, I got this. She was trying to get out with it, but I grabbed it when I had to decide on her or the gun in my side. I decided to address the gun because Callie gets irritated if I track things onto her floor. I'm sure blood would be a big no-no. Anyway, I didn't let go of the pack, and she left without it. It should be interesting to see what she had inside."

As the rest of the team gathered around them, they could hear footsteps and voices approaching. They had to move quickly.

"Everyone, you need to get out of there now," Sharlee ordered.

"She's not wrong, guys. People are beginning to move a little. I've scanned the area for escape routes. Head for the far corner of the lot. That's your best shot."

They moved as a unit, Mark taking point while Carter and Levi covered their rear. The rest flanked Ryker and Oakley, who he kept close, supporting her weakened body with his strength. Another brawny operative came up on the other side of Oakley and supported her, making travel across the lot much quicker. The danger was far from over, and they all knew the consequences of being caught would be dire.

The team escorted Oakley out as the police secured the area, knowing that this was only the beginning of a larger battle against Audra and her twisted beliefs. They had got just a few followers, but they were on the right trail. They had plenty of background work, and now the police were under no illusions that not only was Ryker not the perpetrator of some horrendous crime, but Jac and his crew had done what they were known to do. Get in, get it done, and get out.

"I'll be checking on Dr. Addison in the hospital later," said the person in charge.

Ryker nodded as he climbed into the back of the ambulance. He was never so glad that Sharlee and Kaden were as good as they were, and Monroe knew his stuff on the strategic planning. Without that support, this would have gone FUBAR, and there wouldn't have been much they could have done. Jac and his guys were more than good, but when the number of people tripled after the diversion, they knew there was another place practically next door, housing so many more fanatics.

Oakley clung to Ryker's strong frame, her body trembling and her heart pounding. The dimly lit hideout seemed to close in on her as they made their way out, the cold concrete floor sending shivers up her spine. She could still hear the echoes of

Audra's deranged rantings in her head, but the warmth of Ryker's arms around her was a beacon of safety in the chaos.

"Are you hurt?" Ryker asked Oakley softly, his voice laced with concern. He searched her face for any signs of injury, knowing that she had been through hell and back at the hands of Audra's fanatical followers.

"Nothing serious," Oakley replied, her voice barely audible. "But my mind feels... scattered." Her thoughts were intangible, slipping through her fingers like sand. But as long as Ryker was there, she knew she'd be okay.

"Let's get you checked out by the medics," Sharlee suggested, noticing the cuts and bruises on Oakley's wrists from the restraints. The team had sustained their own injuries during the rescue—Mark had a gash on his arm, while Callie sported a black eye that Garrett was spitting mad about—but their priority was ensuring Oakley's wellbeing.

"Hush Garrett. I'm telling you that while he got in that sucker punch, Ivy would have been impressed with my round-house kick."

Garrett leaned down and kissed her soundly. "I'm impressed too, baby."

"Audra's followers truly believe that medication is causing more harm than good," Jac mused, shaking his head in disbelief. "How can they be so blind to the benefits of proper treatment?"

"Desperation can make people cling to dangerous ideas," Oakley murmured, her eyes distant. "I just hope we can show them there's another way, a better way."

"Oakley's right," Ryker agreed. "But we need to be prepared for the potential dangers of this anti-medication movement. We've seen firsthand what they're capable of."

"Ryker, promise me one thing," Oakley said, her voice quivering with emotion as she met his gaze. "Promise me you won't let Audra destroy everything we've built together. I'm going to have some hard days ahead. Please be patient with me as I work through them."

"Sweetling, there isn't anything that I wouldn't do for you and nothing that can stop me from loving you," Ryker vowed, his blue eyes filled with love. "Nothing and no one will come between us."

She gave him a smile. "I'm depending on that."

As Oakley sat in the back of the ambulance, wrapped in a shock blanket as a paramedic cleaned and bandaged the abrasions on her wrists, the surrounding noise faded into the background. Though the wounds were superficial, a bone-deep ache remained, a reminder of her captivity. She had worked with enough trauma victims, and she had enough training to know this was going to take a while to get over. How long, she hadn't a clue.

Ryker sat beside her, his fingers entwined with hers. His presence was a balm, easing her frayed nerves. It hadn't been easy to convince the first EMT to allow him to sit back there, but when the driver saw who it was, he told his partner that whatever Dr. Addison needed, she got. She had helped him through a bad time in his life. He would be forever grateful. Oakley smiled absently at the gentleman, but at that moment, she couldn't recall him.

"I'm sorry. I don't remember your name or our sessions. It would appear I've had my brains scrambled, but when I do remember you, know I'll be thankful for your kindness."

"You helped me when I didn't think I could be helped. In a small way, I'm paying it forward. Now let's get you some help. Yeah? And Doc? No thanks necessary."

With Ryker near, the panic that threatened to overtake her receded, held at bay by the solid warmth of his body and the steadfast devotion in his eyes.

"How are you feeling?" Ryker asked softly. His thumb traced circles over her knuckles, grounding her in the moment.

"Better now that you're here." Oakley leaned into him, comforted by his familiar scent. "I don't know what I would have done if..." She inhaled a stuttered breath.

"Shh." Ryker pressed a gentle kiss to her temple. "Don't think about that. I'm here now, and I'm not going anywhere."

Oakley closed her eyes, letting his words wash over her. Ryker was her safe harbor in the storm, the one person who could quiet the tumult in her mind. With him, the lingering terror and panic faded, for the moment, into the background, overpowered by his presence.

As long as Ryker was by her side, she knew she would be okay.

The hospital, who knew Dr. Addison because of her work with mutual patients, was gentle and kind to her. Oakley was tired, and when the staff wanted to send Ryker home, he made it known that he went home when his Oakley did. The nurses thought it was sweet.

He wasn't doing it to gain any smiles; he did it because he couldn't do anything else. This woman was his all, and the come-hither looks of women in the hospital, whether an employee, patient, or visitor, irritated him. He used to smile back and make a snap decision if a woman was worth his time to pursue, but now, things were different. He belonged to Oakley, and while he knew others didn't immediately realize he had committed to her, it still irked him.

It was almost a relief that the Med/Surg nurse manager, who was attractive but immune to his charm, was less impressed with his statement. But after explaining the situation to the house supervisor, Ryker was allowed to stay to ease Oakley's distress. Ryker had no illusions about the road ahead. He expected this was one of many things he would have to protect Oakley from and battle for them both. Bring it. He'd gone head-to-head with foreign governments for a cause and moral rights. He'd stand before the Almighty if Oakley needed him to, without hesitation.

Oakley, wrapped in Ryker's arms in a hospital bed, finally relaxed enough to sleep. And for the first time since she had gone missing, he did too.

Chapter 11

Oakley slowly opened her eyes as the harsh glare of the fluorescent lights assaulted her vision. Fear blazed through her body, raising the rhythm of her breathing. She slowly looked around with her eyes first before shifting her head slightly. Something, no, someone warm, was holding onto her hand.

Her head was pounding, the effects of the sedatives and psychotropics still lingering in her system, but she smelled disinfectant and cleanliness. Something had changed. Then she remembered Ryker. Hospital. She was in a hospital. She had something she needed to tell him that was important. But what? Why couldn't she remember? Drugs. Shards of memories were reappearing, but not enough to create a clear block of thought except one. Ryker.

She tried to sit up and nearly vomited, her stomach roiling in protest. She gasped. "Oh, God. I can't."

Oakley took a few deep breaths, willing the nausea to pass. What had they done to her? Flashes of memory surfaced—the sting of a needle piercing her skin, the sickly sweet yet bitter chemical taste in her mouth as they forced her to swallow pills. She gagged.

"Easy there." A firm yet gentle hand supported her back, helping her into a sitting position. Ryker. "Okay, sweetheart.

I've got you. Do you need more anti-nausea medication?" It was about all they could give her, but he was thankful for that small mercy.

She blinked up at him, her eyes glassy. "What happened?" Her voice came out hoarse and weak.

Ryker's face was etched with concern, his blue eyes shadowed. "I'm so sorry, Oakley." His hand tightened around hers. "Charles' sister Audra kidnapped and drugged you. The doctor said we found you just in time."

The memories came flooding back—the van pulling up beside her, a cloth reeking of chemicals pressed over her mouth and nose, and her futile struggles as she was overpowered and injected with drugs. She shuddered, bile rising in her throat.

Ryker grabbed a wastebasket and held it under her chin as she retched. When the spasms had passed, he eased her back against the pillows. "I'm here for you. I won't let anyone hurt you again." His voice was fierce with promise as he offered her water to rinse her mouth and cool her throat.

Oakley stared up at him, her lower lip trembling. "They were going to kill me, weren't they?"

Ryker's jaw clenched. "We aren't sure, but we certainly can't rule it out. I was out of my mind with worry. I won't let them touch you again, and I'm so damn sorry it ever happened at all." He brushed a stray lock of hair from her glistening face, his touch feather-light. "You're safe now. I've got you."

A sob welled up in Oakley's chest as the full impact of her trauma hit her. Ryker wrapped his arms around her, holding her close as she wept against his chest. She clung to him, drawing strength from his solid presence. However long it took, he would help her recover from this. She wasn't alone anymore.

Oakley tried to corral her thoughts, and while he hated how arduous the task was for her, he and the team were desperate for any clue, any word or memory that would give them what they needed, but there weren't many.

"I'm sorry. I feel I have so much important stuff to share, but it's out of reach."

"Don't try too hard, baby, because it can hinder your recovery. When it's time, it will come out."

"What if it doesn't?" she whispered.

"You'll remember what is safe to remember. The rest is unnecessary." Ryker pulled her into his arms for a solid, soul-healing hug. Then he backed up and firmed his voice. "You have a little broth here, and trust me when I say you won't be going home if you can't eat the broth."

Ryker made sure Oakley saw the twinkle in his eye, and when she sighed dramatically, he barely hid his smile. "I guess I'll have to try."

"That's my good girl."

Three days later, Oakley received her walking papers, and the nightmare, part one, was over.

Ryker helped Oakley into the passenger seat of his SUV, concern etching lines into his forehead. Though she insisted she was fine physically, the haunted look in her eyes told a different story. He knew the mental trauma of her kidnapping would take time to heal.

Oakley turned to him with a wistful smile. "How did I get so lucky to have you in my life?"

Warmth flooded Ryker's chest, along with a surge of determination. He would do whatever it took to banish the shadows from Oakley's eyes and keep that radiant smile on her face. "I'm the lucky one. You're the light that brightens my world."

Her smile widened into a grin. "Even after all we've been through, you still have a way with words, Counselor."

"It's a gift." Ryker's lips quirked up at the corners. "But seriously, we're in this together. We'll get through this, just like we get through everything else—with love and faith in each other."

Oakley sighed contentedly and rested her head on his shoulder. "As long as we have that, nothing else matters."

The car ride was more taxing than she had imagined. Ryker tried to anticipate her needs and met them immediately. He helped her with her seatbelt.

"Sweetling, just let me do this. You are so exhausted, and the doctor said not only is it expected, but it will also take some time to build up your strength. We have to wait for the medication to finish metabolizing and then wash out. Who knows how long it will take?"

"I know. But knowing the truth and being patient for it to exit my system are two very different things. I'm so angry, and yet, I understand how scared you get when you only hear one side of an issue. It's all you know, so all you believe."

"Baby girl, I don't want you to get upset again over this. Not now. There will be a time you will be ready to tackle whatever the fallout surrounding these things is, but for now, you rest."

"I like it when you call me baby girl."

Ryker kissed her temple and then her lips gently. When they walked along the complex path to the elevator, she leaned into him, and it boosted his ego.

"Then I guess that's my permission. Many women hate that endearment, and I hesitated. I won't anymore." He observed the condo complex they were entering. "I wonder if we should go into a safe house until this is cleared from your system and we can reassess the danger?"

"Can we talk about it? I'm not sure that will be the best route for me."

Once they were in the condo and Oakley was settled on the sofa with a blanket and a cup of Lady Grey tea in one hand, he drew her close to cuddle on the other side. "Talk to me. What's going on in that brilliant mind of yours?"

Oakley was silent for a long moment, "I can't stop thinking about Audra's followers. The fanaticism in their eyes, the utter conviction that they were doing the right thing. It terrifies me that there are people so opposed to reason and science."

"Unfortunately, there will always be extremists in the world. But for every one of Audra's followers, there are a hundred reasonable people who support our cause." Ryker gave her hand a comforting squeeze. "We can't control the radicals. We can only continue to spread our message of hope and healing. With knowledge and understanding, we can overcome ignorance and fear."

Ryker sat her teacup on the side table to make way for his arms to come around her, holding her close.

Ryker felt the tension ease from Oakley's body as a sense of peace settled over them. The future was unclear, but their bond was strong.

A thrill went through Oakley at the implied threat in Ryker's words. She knew how formidable he and his team could be, and she took a savage satisfaction in the thought of Audra and her followers getting what they deserved.

Ryker's arms tightened around her, and she gave herself to the peace and comfort of his embrace. The threat of Audra and her followers seemed distant now, held at bay by the strength of Ryker's love. She knew how to change her thinking and could do it as long as they were together, Oakley knew she had nothing to fear and yet, there was still it remained in the back of her mind.

Oakley leaned into Ryker, drawing comfort from his solid presence. She breathed in his scent, felt the steady beat of his heart against her cheek. Here, in his embrace, she felt safe. Protected. Loved.

"What are we going to do about Audra?" she asked. "She's still out there, and she won't stop. She'll keep coming after me to further her cause."

Ryker's jaw tightened. "We won't let her get near you again. Jac's group is working with the police to track Audra and her followers. We'll find them, and we'll put a stop to this once and for all."

"Be careful," Oakley said. "Audra is unhinged, and her followers are fanatics. I remember hearing them getting almost uncontrollable when she would talk to them. It sounded like a radical cult or something. They won't go down without a fight. They don't seem to be worried about being the sacrifice. There is just so much wrong here. And..."

"What's wrong? Did you remember something?"

Oakley shook her head hesitantly. "I have something that I need to remember. Something important, but I can't seem to track it down in my brain. Oh! It's just so frustrating."

Ryker pulled her close, and she laid her head on his chest. "It will be okay. I promise it will work out. Don't force it, or you will lose it. Slow and easy."

"Don't worry about us, or rather Jac's crew." Ryker cupped her face in his hands, gazing at her intently. "Your safety is my top priority. Audra made a mistake by threatening you. Now she'll face the full force of my friend's capabilities."

"Promise me you won't go back into that battlefield."

"No, I can't promise, but it isn't my intention. I'm staying in as part of the group, planning and strategizing, but I'm not going to confront anyone because, unlike Jac and his people, my best playground is the courtroom."

"There's no need to dwell on Audra right now," he said. "You're safe here with me. We have this moment together, and that's what matters."

Oakley smiled, leaning in to steal another kiss. "You're right. Being with you is all I need."

THE NEXT AFTERNOON, Ryker and Oakley sat in his living room; cups of tea cradled in their hands. Though Oakley didn't show much in the way of outward physical harm, it had devastated her mental and physical health, and that shook her to the core. She was hypervigilant, and her sleep had been snatches of dozing rather than a full restful sleep. Ryker refused to leave her alone, insisting she stay with him until she felt safe again.

"What if that is never?" Oakley whispered.

"It's too early to ask that question, baby. You are staying here until we are both comfortable with you being alone, and, to be honest, I don't think I'll ever be okay with that. Couldn't you just move in?"

"I could, for the short term, and then later we can discuss it again. Okay?"

"I'll take it. I'll get some guys to grab what you need from your place later in the week."

She smiled her relief. "Thank you for understanding. I don't know if I will go back for a while, but for right now, I'm not going to leave this apartment for the foreseeable future."

"That's fine by me. I've gotten great at working from home, and unless I'm headed to the courtroom, I'm able to see clients virtually. Something you could do in the future." She gave him a distressed look. "Or not."

"My lease is up in two months. I need to give notice. I don't think I'll be able to return that soon."

Ryker could see it was causing her immense distress to consider returning to seeing patients or the business side of things. He was a fixer, and helping her get things settled for now was in his wheelhouse.

"I'll get that typed up for you." He grinned. "Rather, I'll get Mara to do that."

"Thank you. Oh! Shandra. What about her? She must be crazy by now. Did she get a new job?"

Ryker hesitated before taking in a big breath and letting it out slowly. "Well, this is what I did to put a bandage on that issue." He explained his rescue plan and then patted her hand. "You are welcome to take her back to do your business side of things, but I don't think I'd recommend it."

"No, she was mediocre on her good days. But do you need another employee?"

Ryker grimaced. "No, Mara, my office manager, runs a tight ship, and, as a personal assistant, I have to admit, Shandra is rather lazy. She didn't even know how to use Excel very well, nor did she bill properly. I took your last six months' information over to my biller, and she is going back to bill those not sent to insurance. We might want to look at your accounts further back later. You made a lot more than you were realizing."

Oakley frowned. "I had wondered but chalked it up to slow insurance payments. What are we going to do?"

"I'll let her go, saying it didn't work out and you are not re-opening your office anytime soon. I'll give her two weeks paid so she can use that time to find another job without losing pay."

"You are so kind."

"I will never be confused with someone who is kind except around you. I have a reputation for being hard-nosed. Ruthless, even."

She patted his hand. "Your secret is safe with me."

He kissed her lips, deepening it as she drew him closer. Before she was completely satisfied, he pulled back. "Time for a nap, baby. You need your rest. Everything you feel you've lost will come back. Promise."

With kisses like that, she could believe he was right. She allowed him to settle her on the sofa for a quick nap while Ryker worked. It turned into three hours. She didn't wake up once. That was progress.

That night, Oakley cuddled in with Ryker in his bed, hoping sleep would come. No medications until her system had nothing left. That might be a little while, so she settled in for some perpetual nights, but so long as she had Ryker near her, she would get through.

Finally, Oakley gave up the pretense of falling asleep. It just wasn't happening. Ryker was reading, but she couldn't concentrate enough to read. Looking at the profile of this amazing man, she readily admitted he was more than she had ever dreamed of having, and she wasn't going to give him up without a fight. He was her knight, her voice of reason, and her patient lover. She understood that men released tension easily, but most women were more emotional. Unfortunately, her emotional stability was all over the place. She felt the tingles of love deeply and a little arousal, but not the desire to consummate.

Hopefully, it wouldn't take long for her sense of safety to be restored enough to fall into sexual abandon with Ryker. Their sexy times were what romance novels wrote about, but now?

"How could Audra do this?" Oakley whispered. "She was once a compassionate woman who cared for her brother when he needed her most. Oh, maybe that was it. He had been doing so well that he wouldn't need her to care for him any longer. Her usefulness would be a thing of the past where her brother was concerned. Her fears turned to anger and resentment. Now she's turned into this... this monster."

"Her beliefs have become an obsession," Ryker said grimly. "She's so convinced that she's right, she can't see the harm she's causing. She needs help, but she'll never accept it."

"If she'd just agree to proper treatment, medication along with therapy could help her. But she's too far gone to see reason. Honestly, just treatment that included therapy might work." Oakley sighed, staring into the depths of his eyes. "I don't know if there's any way to reach people so committed to their delusions. My experience says to treat it differently, but she is dangerous, and those who follow her."

"We have to try whenever we are given the opportunity. Obstacles are just something to find a way around." Ryker swept a swath of hair off her face. "Educating people about mental health and the benefits of medication is the only way to counter these anti-science movements. We can't force treatment on those who refuse it, nor should we, but we can spread the truth. Hopefully, that will dispel the lies groups like this one are spreading. It's frightening to those who have no real understanding of the issue."

A yawn signaled a chance to snatch a few hours before a nightmare woke her. She snuggled into Ryker after he turned off the light and slid down under the cover. Soon she would go back to the doctor for more tests. Hopefully, things would get better soon.

Chapter 12

Oakley woke with a start, her heart pounding. For a moment, she didn't recognize her surroundings. Bella was immediately on her mind. Audra was the second thought. Then she felt the warmth of Ryker's body curled around hers and remembered—she was in his bed, safe in his embrace.

She took a deep, steadying breath, trying to calm her frayed nerves. But the memory of rough hands dragging her into the van and a needle piercing her skin kept replaying in her mind. She shuddered, a lump forming in her throat.

Ryker stirred behind her. "Nightmare?" His voice was rough with sleep.

Oakley nodded. "The same one."

He pulled her closer, his arms tightening around her in a comforting hug. "I'm here. You're safe."

She took another deep breath, absorbing his warmth and strength. But while she knew Ryker would protect her with his life, she couldn't escape the lingering fear and helplessness that had taken root inside her. And that fear was being fueled by a single text that had popped up on her phone two days ago.

Audra: I'm still out here. Watching and waiting.

Then yesterday, another came through.

Audra: Do you think you are safe in your fancy attorney's home?

Oakley hadn't told Ryker about the messages. She didn't want him to worry, didn't want him to put his life on hold to guard her every second of the day. But Audra's threat meant Oakley couldn't escape what had happened. She would live in fear for the foreseeable future, constantly watching over her shoulder for any signs of danger unless she shared with Ryker so he could protect her. Before this happened, she would have ignored it and gone on. Now, she was terrified. She had to tell him.

Ryker kissed the top of her head. "Try to get some more rest." His voice was laced with concern. His tone told her he didn't believe for a second that she was fine, even if she told him otherwise. "Your appointment with the therapist is this afternoon."

Oakley bit her lip. She wasn't looking forward to rehashing the details of her trauma again. But she had to get past this and find a way to move on from the darkness that seemed intent on consuming her, for Ryker's sake and her own. The person they had chosen was someone she respected.

"I know," she whispered.

And she would go, if only to ease the worry in Ryker's eyes. She owed him that much. He had saved her life, after all. Now it was time for her to fight for her own happiness. Her kidnapper had already taken too much from her. She wouldn't let Audra win.

"Ryker, I need to show you something."

"Baby, you need to get more sleep."

"I can't right now. I'll take a nap later." He looked skeptical. Smart man. "Promise."

"Okay. What do you need to show me?"

OAKLEY SPENT THE MORNING resting in bed while Ryker worked from home, only leaving her side to make them both lunch. The medication left her groggy and disoriented, and today, she drifted in and out of a fitful sleep. When she was awake, her thoughts kept circling back to her time in captivity, the feeling of helplessness and terror that had threatened to overtake her.

She was living in a world of life clips, some longer, some shorter. She could dream more vividly than she ever had, yet she couldn't always retain more than a feeling of terror. And tied up with those scrambled thoughts was Bella. Where was she, and why had she disappeared on the same day that Oakley did? And why was she in her dreams?

She'd shown Ryker the texts, and her recollection of that conversation was clear.

"You got these before today."

His calm statement of fact made her cringe. She was a confident woman, but right now, she depended on Ryker for everything. It was maddening and comforting. He loved her. He showed it in so many ways, and logically, she understood her mental motivation, but it wasn't enough to assuage the guilt or the anger. She cherished her feelings of being cared for and was angry she had to rely so heavily on another person to do what she had done for herself entirely due to another's actions.

Cognitively, she processed that she was trying to avoid more mental strain and trauma and that letting Ryker in on what was going on would ultimately do that, but emotionally, it was another story altogether. She was devastated that she was in this frame of mind and was feeling guilty that this wasn't what he had signed up for.

Ryker sat beside her, his large hand enveloping hers as if he could chase the demons away through his touch alone.

"I'm here," he kept repeating softly. "You're safe now." When his sweetness seemed to rub salt in her wounds, he stopped. "Whatever you're thinking, stop." His no-nonsense tone helped her drag her thinking back to level ground. "I want to be here, with you. I choose you and whatever comes with you."

"Physically, maybe. But mentally, I may never be truly safe again." Her tears ran down her cheeks. "I'm trying."

"I know, baby girl. Typically, I'm not a big touchy-feely guy, but with you, I seem to have some insight. I want to touch you all the time. I almost feel your pain. It's foreign to me to be tuned in so much to another person, but I'm so glad I am. I think I understand why you might not want to share these messages, but it's the only way I or Jac and his gang can keep on top of this. Let's see if you can do your session virtually, because you aren't leaving this apartment without protection, and I'm not sure I can arrange it fast enough."

"I will call the therapist to change the appointment venue."

"Good. While you do that, I'll put in a call to Jac. I think we need more coverage. Maybe even a change of a resting place while things get worked out."

His steady presence was the only thing grounding her, keeping the panic at bay. She didn't know how she would have survived this without him. Ryker had become her anchor in the churning sea of her emotions, the one thing she could cling to when the memories and anxiety threatened to pull her under. She knew it might get worse before it got better.

The therapist agreed to change to virtual sessions for the time being. Jac was concerned with the text messages. "Jac, it worries me because she knows where Oakley is. I'm not as surprised about that as I am that she is openly stalking her. Taunting her and threatening harm is something I can file on. The problem is, if we could have found her, we would have by now. I'm calling the detective after this."

"I need you two here. It's safer and better protected than your building, even with the security you have. You might be met with resistance, but once Oakley sees things are easier and more secure here, she will agree. She's a smart woman and wouldn't allow her desire for familiar surroundings to keep her from being safe. That is more important and will ultimately make her relax."

"I agree. I want her wrapped in as much protection as possible. That way, when I need to go to court or get some things signed or whatever, I can do that with confidence. We will have still wrapped her securely."

"So make your call to the detective and let me know when you are coming. I'll put out the word. Guess it's a family night tonight."

Ryker clicked off and thought about his friend's need to have his family close. It was that damned control issue he always had going strong. This was always who Jac had been with his guys in the military, and his employees in the agency. What was his was his. Suddenly it clicked with Ryker that while he'd always laughed and just dismissed Jac's need to be within arm's reach of his people, it was that same need that Ryker now had with Oakley.

He needed her protected by mouthy but intelligent, skill-laden men who would die defending what was theirs. He was lucky he had these kinds of men within arm's reach and that they counted him and Oakley among their numbers as family. With new relief and resolve, he put in the call to the detective.

Detective Linton, one of Jac's military buddies, was on the force and often helped when needed. He couldn't do much for them while she was a missing person, but now that Oakley had given a statement that Audra and her group kidnapped her, things had changed. Linton had snagged the case. His captain often assigned Jac's cases to him for continuity and because Jacquard Reynaud tended to be a dog with a bone. Linton could handle that.

Linton listened to Ryker and agreed to meet at Jac's place later this afternoon, after Oakley's session. "She needs to be as protected as possible. Jac can provide that for her and you."

"I don't need it."

"Don't be so sure, my friend. If they are trying to make a point, they have already made it with Oakley about her personal safety and the effects of medications. Now, to get to her in a way that will hurt forever, they need to get to you."

CONVINCING OAKLEY THAT more was better in the protection and bodyguard department was easier than he thought, and Ryker was relieved that she accepted it immediately. "Not that I don't think you can't handle everything," she said as she cupped his cheek in her hand. "I don't want you to have to. The courtroom is your battleground, remember?"

"I'm worried about you dealing with all of this."

She shook her head. "I'll be okay." Ryker knew her words sounded braver than she felt. "I need to test the lines of my security, or it will bind me rather than free me."

He hesitated, clearly torn between giving her space and ensuring her safety. "But leaving the security of even this apartment is a challenge."

Oakley placed her hand against his cheek again. "It is, but you'll be right next to me, supporting me. I know that."

Ryker leaned down and kissed her softly. "Always."

The single word was filled with meaning, a promise that went beyond this moment. Oakley drew strength from it as she walked through the doors of her cocoon, clinging to the knowledge that Ryker would be there to catch her if she fell.

When it was time to go to Jac's house, Levi, Callie, and Garrett arrived to get them there.

"Why so many of you?" asked an alarmed Oakley.

"I have to drive my rig because I anticipate needing to run into court or work sometimes."

Callie smiled. "We have already moved your car to the underground garage at the shop."

"What shop?" asked Oakley.

"Sorry. The office. I call it the shop because going to the office doesn't appeal to me." Callie shrugged.

"Oh... right. I've always loved saying I'm going to the office. That's a good idea, I guess," said Oakley. "But why?"

Garrett explained. "See, we can stop any tracking being done on your vehicle once it's in the garage. We can also sweep it for any devices and clean them off, so when you're ready to drive it, you won't have to worry."

"Um, I guess you're right. I'll want to drive sometime."

Ryker pulled her close. "But that is in the future and nothing to be concerned about right now."

Levi clapped his hands, and Oakley jumped. "Damn. Sorry, Oakley. Didn't get enough coffee today, I guess."

"Or too much," grumbled Garrett. "Levi is riding with you, Ryker. Callie and I will bring Oakley."

"Oh, but... I," The panic was rising as Oakley's breathing hitched and picked up.

"Change of plans. Callie, you ride with Levi in Ryker's car. Ryker and Oakley will ride with me."

Ryker squeezed Oakley tighter. "Deep breaths, baby girl. Slow and easy, now. I won't leave you."

"Okay," she said. "I'm sorry I'm such a coward."

"Shit, girl. You are anything but that. Who wouldn't want the hunk in their life to be by their side when they're freaked out? It's all good."

"We'll follow you to Jac's, then take this rig off to the garage to have it swept before I bring it out to you."

"Sound's good. Thanks," said Ryker.

"LEVI JUST CALLED. OAKLEY'S rig was clear of tracking devices, but Ryker's had one."

"I knew it," said Linton. "She's after Ryker."

"Damn, the man's right," said Monroe. "That would be an excellent strategy. If Audra threatens Oakley, you'd be more worried about her, stand closer, protect her harder, and not worry about yourself, thinking the only danger lies with Oakley. When, in fact, they are targeting you."

"Shit. Now how do I do all that I need to do, take care of Oakley, and watch out for myself?" Ryker's hand ravaged his longer-than-typical hair, leaving it standing on end.

Monroe nodded. "That's the point, except she doesn't know you have us to stand in the gap."

"Yes, okay, but what does that mean in this case?"

"We protect you both," said Jac. "Not brain surgery."

"Fuck," said Ryker. "I'm glad the girls are here and are keeping her busy. This would kill her right now."

"Sorry, but it just answers my question of how we deal with the situation. We cover you both. I want you two here, and as much as possible, you work here. If you have to leave, then we will take care of that with a bodyguard and a tail."

"Great," said Ryker unenthusiastically.

Monroe jumped into operation mode. "Now, how do we want this game to play out?"

The men put their heads together and devised a plan.

THE COLD WIND WHIPPED Oakley's hair around her face as she stood on the rooftop terrace, clutching the railing with trembling hands. Her heart pounded in her chest, a chaotic rhythm that echoed the confusion and fear swirling through her mind. The medication that had been administered to her during her harrowing ordeal may not still course through her veins, but she was still unsteady and weak at times.

"Oakley?" Ryker's voice was gentle, filled with concern as he approached her from behind. "Are you okay?"

She shook her head, tears filling her sad eyes. "I don't know, Ryker. I don't know if I'll ever be okay again."

Ryker stepped closer, his hand hovering just above her shoulder, hesitant to touch her after all she'd been through. "Do you want to talk about it? What happened?"

Oakley swallowed hard, trying to find the words to describe the nightmare she'd endured. The memories were sharp, like shards of glass slicing into her psyche whenever she tried to look back. "I was... they took me," she whispered, her voice shaking with the effort to speak. "They kept me in this... this filthy room, and they... they drugged me. They kept pumping me full of this horrible stuff that made me feel like I was losing my mind, and I couldn't escape, no matter how hard I tried."

Her free hand unconsciously went up to twirl a strand of hair, a nervous habit she'd developed over the years. "They hurt me, Ryker. Physically, emotionally... I've never felt so helpless and alone in my entire life."

Ryker's face contorted with anguish, struggling to comprehend the depth of her pain. "Oh, Oakley," he breathed, finally placing a comforting hand on her shoulder. "I'm so sorry. I wish there was something I could have done to protect you."

She leaned into his touch, seeking solace in the warmth of his presence. "It's not your fault," she murmured. "But I don't know how I'm supposed to heal from this."

"Time," he told her softly, wrapping an arm around her and pulling her close. "You need time, Oakley. And I'll be here with you every step of the way, I promise."

As they stood together on that windswept rooftop, Oakley allowed herself a small measure of hope. With Ryker by her side, perhaps the road to recovery wouldn't be quite so lonely.

And maybe, just maybe, she could find her way back to the strong, confident woman she'd once been–before the darkness had stolen her away.

"Thank you, Ryker," she whispered, her voice barely audible over the howling wind. "I don't know what I would do without you."

"Nor I you," he admitted, his own voice tinged with emotion. "Nor I you."

The faint, incessant beep of a text message notification rang through the bedroom like an alarm, causing her heart to race. Ryker's protective gaze scanned the room before he reached for her phone on the coffee table. His jaw clenched as he read the message from an unknown number.

"Oakley, it's Audra again," he said, his voice strained. "She's still harassing you. She must have found a way to bypass the security measures we put in place."

"Let me see," Oakley demanded, her frustration mounting as she snatched the phone from his hand. The message displayed a sinister smiley face emoji followed by the words, "You may have escaped once, but I'll find you again, Dr. Addison."

"Ryker, I can't take this anymore. Between the medication, trying to recover, and now Audra... it feels like I'm being suffocated."

Ryker's eyes filled with concern, knowing that he had played a part in her feelings of constraint. He had become incredibly protective since her kidnapping, driving her to appointments, and keeping her car at the underground parking garage at Jac's agency. Part of him felt responsible for not initiating immediate protocols after knowing Oakley dealt with many at-risk members of society.

"Oakley, I know that my protectiveness might be overwhelming, but I cannot allow anything like that to happen to you again. I promise I will do whatever it takes to keep you safe."

"Thank you, Ryker," Oakley sighed, rubbing her temples. "But I need space, too. I need to find a balance between healing and feeling trapped. Can we work together to figure this out?"

"Of course," he agreed, his voice softening. "I promise to give you the space you need while ensuring Audra is stopped."

As Ryker drove Oakley to her next appointment, their thoughts were consumed with the weight of everything that had transpired. Oakley's mind raced with memories of her harrowing experience and her current frustration at her slower-than-desired recovery. Ryker couldn't shake his guilt for not doing more to protect her from the start.

"Ryker," Oakley began hesitantly, "I appreciate your protection, but I need you to understand that I'm strong too. I survived that ordeal, and I will survive this."

He looked over at her, admiration shining in his eyes. "I know you're strong, Oakley. I've always known that. But it doesn't change the fact that I want to do everything I can to keep you safe."

"I know Jac and his group are trying to find and bring Audra to justice, but I think, if I'm to heal, I have to be part of the solution that ends that woman's reign," she said with quiet resolution. "It will allow my brain to believe she is out of circulation, and it will put an end to my feeling of helplessness. I need to breathe free air again, and I fear that won't happen if I don't have a part in her demise."

Ryker held his response for a moment and concentrated on traffic. When the cars thinned out, he said, "Sweetling, I hear what you're saying, but I need to clarify. You want to be part of the planning but not the actual takedown, right? Because I don't know that I'll participate in that. It isn't my specialty like it is Jac's people's."

"Part of me would love to see it, and maybe Sharlee will be happy to let me watch from her computer, but no, I don't think that being there is as important as knowing I was part of the reason Audra lost. Gives me my power back."

"I understand that. Deal," he agreed, gripping her hand that was lying in her lap. "I'll talk with Jac."

Chapter 13

The sun dipped below the horizon, casting an orange glow across Oakley's face as she stood in one of Jac and Sharlee's lounge rooms, clutching a small potted plant. Her fingers traced the delicate veins of the leaves, a silent reminder of life and growth amidst the chaos that had become her reality. As she looked out the window, she couldn't help but feel disconnected from the world outside.

"Oakley?" Ryker's voice cut through her thoughts, soft but insistent. He stood at the doorway, watching her with concern etched into his strong features.

"Sorry," she murmured, setting the plant down on the windowsill. "I was just... lost in thought."

"Hey, it's okay." He approached her, wrapping his arms around her waist and resting his chin on her shoulder. "How are you feeling today?"

She sighed, leaning back into his embrace. "The medication makes me feel so fuzzy-headed. I can't focus on anything for more than a few minutes. It's frustrating."

"Give it time," he whispered. Your body is still recovering from everything you went through."

"I know. It's just... I want to be better already," she admitted, her voice cracking slightly.

Ryker tightened his hold on her, offering silent support. "Why don't we take a walk? Maybe some fresh air will help clear your head."

"Okay," she agreed hesitantly, allowing him to guide her out of the side door and down the garden path. They walked hand-in-hand, their fingers entwined, as the grounds lights began to flicker on around them.

Their steps slowed when they reached a small pond, its small dock casting eerie shadows in the fading sunlight. Oakley paused, taking deep breaths as she tried to focus her scattered thoughts.

"Being outside helps a little," she conceded, looking up at Ryker with a small smile. "But I can't escape the feeling that I'm not truly safe, even with you by my side and all of this security."

"Oakley," Ryker's voice was firm, his eyes locked on hers. "I will do everything in my power to protect you. You have my word."

"I know you will." She squeezed his hand, her eyes glistening with unshed tears. "It's just... this whole situation has shaken me to my core. I never imagined something like this would happen to me."

"Me neither," he admitted, his voice thick with emotion.

"Ryker," she whispered, suddenly vulnerable. "I need your help to overcome this. I can't do it alone."

"Of course," he vowed, pulling her into a tight embrace. "We'll face this together. We'll heal, and we'll grow stronger from it."

As Oakley leaned into Ryker's comforting arms, she felt the first flicker of hope ignite within her heart. The road ahead would be difficult, but with Ryker by her side, she knew they could face anything.

"Thank you, Ryker," she murmured, pressing her face against his chest. "For everything."

"Anything for you, baby, you know that," he replied, his voice full of love and determination.

RYKER STEELED HIMSELF as he entered the dimly lit conference room, where the team assembled around a large table, their faces determined and focused. The air was thick with tension, each member keenly aware of the stakes involved in finding Audra and uncovering her next plans.

"All right, everyone," Carter said, taking his place at the end of the table. "I'm taking point here, replacing Mark, who needs a break."

Mark snickered good-naturedly. "Whatever you need to tell yourself, man."

Carter slugged Mark playfully in the arm. Carter turned serious again. "We need to stop Audra before she can hurt anyone else. Let's review what we know so far and discuss our next moves."

"Agreed," said Sharlee. She was called the Vapor on the deep web, and as the team's intelligence analyst, she had the uncanny ability to sift through data and connect seemingly unrelated pieces of information. "Audra has been keeping a low profile since Oakley's rescue, but that doesn't mean she's stopped planning her next move."

"Right," chimed in Kaden, the team's hardware and software tech expert. His fingers danced across his laptop keyboard as he pulled up the relevant information on the screen. "I've been monitoring her known associates and digging into any new leads that might point us in the right direction."

"Good man, Kaden," Carter praised, scanning the faces of his team members.

"Now, we also have Ava, our profiler, on loan from Callie's earlier Homeland Security days, who's been working tirelessly to get inside Audra's head and understand her motivations.

"According to Ava," said Callie, "She doesn't think that Audra started out so driven or fanatical. But when her way of life was threatened for a third time in her adult life, it was more than she could handle."

"What do you mean, third time?" asked Carter.

"First, her husband decimated her trust. Ava believes her husband brainwashed Audra into believing she was only good at being a wife when she made her husband happy. She was a convert until Charles found out. He convinced her that the domestic violence she was experiencing in the marriage was unhealthy.

"When her husband wouldn't change, and in fact escalated, he destroyed her worth as a spouse and her faith in him. When her mother left right after she moved back home instead of supporting her, it was another abandonment. Then finally, when Charles' illness was diagnosed and treated with excellent outcomes, someone betrayed her again. She would once again be left alone. And she loved all the other people who had betrayed her, so it had to be turned elsewhere."

"Oakley," said Ryker.

"Yep," said Callie.

"She fixated on her, and it became her entire focus. Becoming fanatical is just another version of her obsessive personality."

Jac spoke into the quiet after the last statement. "Based on Sharlee's analysis combined with Ava's interpretations, Audra is likely feeling cornered and desperate. She'll be more dangerous now than ever before, which means we need to act swiftly and decisively."

"Agreed," Ryker said, his jaw set in determination. "Marco, what have you uncovered during your recon missions?"

"Audra's been careful," Marco admitted, his voice low and confident. "But I've managed to track down a few leads. There's a warehouse on the outskirts of town that's been receiving an unusual amount of traffic lately. It could be worth checking out."

"I got the address and ran the ownership through the computer. We found it belongs to Harry Dergan—a developer who lost his wife to suicide a few years ago. The information I could pull up said she had mental health issues. Evidently, she could not overcome them," said Sharlee.

"Excellent," said Carter, making a note of the location. "We'll need to coordinate our efforts and ensure we're all working together seamlessly. The element of surprise would be nice, but it might not be available to us."

"Well, as we now have Linton, it will be easier," said Monroe.

Linton chuckled. "In theory, yes. But I can't condone any vigilantism. But what law-abiding citizens run into in their normal course of a day is not a problem."

As the team discussed their next moves, Oakley's face flashed in Ryker's mind. He knew the emotional toll her ordeal had taken on her and was determined to bring Audra to justice.

"Okay, team, let's split up and follow these leads," Carter instructed. "We don't have time to mess around. Ryker, Oakley is yours and Levi's. I need someone with a bit more skills than you have, my lawyer friend."

"I agree. But I need to be in on what's happening. Oakley needs closure."

Jac looked at his wife. "Charlotte, continue analyzing the data and look for any patterns that might emerge."

Carter looked at Kaden. "Keep monitoring Audra's associates and cross-reference their movements with the intel Mark and Callie gather. I need you to assess the warehouse, and find who is coming and going from it. Monroe, get the information you need to assess if the warehouse is a viable target, and can we breach it? We will call Ava into play when we have information she can work with. Everyone good?"

"Good," they replied in unison, their faces set with steely resolve.

As the team dispersed, Ryker allowed himself a brief moment of vulnerability, his thoughts turning to Oakley once more. She needed him now more than ever, and he vowed to do everything in his power to protect her and help the guys bring Audra to justice.

The sun had slipped below the horizon as Callie and Mark approached a seemingly abandoned warehouse, its walls covered in graffiti and its windows shattered. The air was thick with the scent of mold and decay, sending a shiver down Callie's spine as she cracked her knuckles.

"This is a perfect Halloween haunted house," said Callie. "Let's get to it and get out. This place is creepy."

"According to Kaden's intel, this is one of the last known locations Audra used," said Callie. "There might be people inside who can tell us more about her whereabouts."

"Let's hope they're willing to talk," Leo replied, his normally jovial demeanor replaced by an unyielding seriousness.

STEPPING THROUGH A rusted metal door, they found themselves in a dimly lit room filled with crates and discarded furniture. A handful of people huddled together, their expressions a mix of fear and defiance. At the sight of Callie and Leo, they visibly stiffened.

"Who are you? What do you want?" a woman demanded, protective of those behind her.

"We just want to ask some questions about Audra," Leo said calmly, hands raised in a non-threatening gesture.

"Audra? What about her?" the woman replied hesitantly, her eyes flickering between Callie's imposing figure and Leo's reassuring smile.

"Let me cut to the chase," Callie interjected, her voice low and menacing. "We know Audra orchestrated Oakley's kidnapping, and we need your help to find her before she hurts anyone else."

"Oakley? That girl didn't deserve what happened to her," another man murmured, breaking the tense silence. "I can't speak for everyone here, but I'm tired of Audra using us like pawns. She promised us protection, but all she's done is put our lives at risk. I lost my job, my family, and my home because she said it was a better life without my medication."

As he spoke, others in the room nodded in agreement, sharing whispered stories of Audra's ruthlessness and manipulation.

"At first," said the woman, "she was kind and helpful. She made it seem like there was a better life off the medication. Then, when it was obvious we were having difficulties, instead of helping us, she left us here to live with our demons."

Mark looked around. "Are you all that is here?"

"The rest wandered off in their fear and demons to some other place," the woman whispered.

"Can I get you to a place where you are cared for and hopefully stabilize your lives again?"

The group murmured and then agreed. Mark called in reinforcements. Callie helped the woman up, and the rest could ambulate alone. The community mental health consortium had a mental health-centered homeless shelter where they got people back on their medication and brought in services to help them re-establish themselves.

"Audra mentioned an upcoming meeting with some new recruits," one man offered, a determined glint in his eyes. "It's happening tomorrow night at an old factory across town."

"Thank you," said Callie. "That is excellent information."

"Stop her," said the woman.

Mark nodded confidently. "We will."

Once the van arrived, they helped the group inside and called Jac.

The stakes were high, and emotions ran even higher as the team prepared to confront Audra. They understood the reasons behind her actions—a twisted desire for power and control—but they refused to let her continue to manipulate and harm others. The grumbling dissent among Audra's followers only fueled their determination as they recognized the opportunity to exploit her weakening grip on her people.

Chapter 14

"**D**o you have to go today?" There was anxiety and fear in Oakley's voice. It wasn't that those emotions were displayed often, but this time it was for Ryker.

"I have to go to court today." She whimpered, which was unusual before the kidnapping but becoming familiar since. "I'll call you before I go in and after I leave so you know I'm safe. I'll have Levi with me, and no one will do anything in the courtroom. That would be a suicide mission."

"If you say so. Are you sure just Levi is enough? I mean, Carter..." she shrugged.

"Yes, Carter is a big guy, and his presence is more intimidating, but I don't want to intimidate everyone in a courtroom. Don't underestimate Levi. He has plenty of skills."

"I know, it's just..." she shrugged.

"Oakley, baby, come here." He drew her into his arms. "I'm going to be fine. Everything will go as planned, and I'll be back as soon as I'm through winning my case."

"That could take a while."

"It could, but I'm good, remember, so it shouldn't take long at all. I'll be home by four."

Oakley murmured her response into his shirt, and he pulled her closer and hugged her tightly. "It will be fine."

She nodded and took a deep breath before pushing away from his chest and taking a step back.

"I've got to go. Living this far from work sure puts a cramp in my schedule."

Oakley laughed. "Um, pretty sure, that's a cramp in your style."

"Nope, my style is fine. It's my damn schedule that is off. It just makes me late, stressed about timeframes in the morning and when I'm irritated first thing, the rest of the day is going downhill. It's like leaving sixty minutes before court instead of thirty to make sure I am there on time."

"Mmm, okay," she said with a shake of her head. "For what it's worth, I like your style too."

Dropping another kiss on her lips, Ryker stood back so Oakley could walk out of the room ahead of him and, with one final smile of encouragement, went down the stairs. He passed Callie, who said something to Oakley in a cheerful voice. He heard some of the women's names and was grateful for their taking Oakley under their wing.

His Oakley was taking the enforced seclusion from the world well. In fact, if he were to make a further statement, he might say she was relieved to be here under lock and key and guard. He wondered if he would ever get the confident, fiery woman back that he had before the kidnapping. He loved her and made no excuses about that fact, but he did want her to enjoy her life. Tracking and looking for Audra would not produce security and confidence in anyone, especially Oakley. This had to come to an end soon.

Riding in the passenger seat of the well-appointed Escalade belonging to the agency's fleet, Ryker almost wished that Audra would make a move. If she did make one, then that would force everyone's hand. They would be able to stop her, arrest her, and put her group under notice. That would allow the rest of them to begin to put the pieces back together and return to the life they had before she disrupted everything.

Ryker took a deep breath and let it slowly out, calming his mind and clearing it of all the personal things he had to deal with in favor of concentrating on his client and the court case. His officer client had been discharged without proper due process because if that had been done, it would be obvious that when they asked him to terminate his commission, they would have known that what they were accusing him of did not happen. It didn't take Ryker long to figure that out, and it wouldn't have taken internal affairs any longer.

Besides asking for the decision to be overturned, Ryker was also asking for compensation and his legal bill to be paid by the government. He knew just how to do it because he had done it plenty of times before, and was well known in certain circles for his thoroughness and accuracy.

Ryker was also well-known for declining cases. When he started to get into the cases and found out they weren't accurate and appropriate, he wouldn't represent the client. He wasn't there to make money, although of course, he needed to make it. He was doing this particular angle of advocacy because few other attorneys were. And because it was his passion.

A passion just like Oakley had a passion for the mental health of these same people. He wondered how many of these clients he and Oakley had cross-served over the years. She would have had to help after he had won their case; otherwise, he would have seen her name before he met her. He was a thorough researcher, and so was his intern researcher. They would have run into Oakley's name if she had been working with any of the clients before or simultaneously with him.

Levi pulled the Escalade into the parking area of the courthouse, driving him to a space near the elevator.

"I don't usually get the opportunity to have someone drive me to court, escort me in, and hang out while I'm brilliant in front of the judge."

"Yeah, whatever, man, I'm just here because I was told to be. Your brilliance isn't something I'm particularly eager to see, if you know what I mean."

"Asshole."

"Hey, just being honest here." Levi laughed at the face Ryker was giving him, causing Ryker to laugh as well.

"OK, let's go get this over with so I can get back to Oakley."

Levi remarked as they entered the elevator, "You really love her."

Looking ahead, he replied, "I really do."

Levi shook his head. "I thought I would need to bow out with Finley because of you. We're just friends and all, but I like going out and doing things with her, but you are tough competition. You have the money to do whatever you want to do. It isn't that I'm not without resources, but it's hard to beat classy, rich, and handsome."

They got off the elevator, and Ryker looked at his watch before checking the area around them. He led Levi off to the side of the broad entranceway.

"Finley doesn't care about those things. She is a little rough around the edges too, and the two of you have similar tastes. I like a tablecloth on the table, and she'd eat lunch standing if it suited her needs."

Levi cocked his head to the side. "She's less bothered with conventions, and you like them."

"Well, more than Finley does. Besides, I want a wife and a family. Finley would likely be fine with the wife part, but kids are not in her plans."

"She's Storm's nanny, so I get not wanting to have more to take care of. I'm not much of a kid person, either. I mean, I like them, but," he shrugged.

"And that right there is a big reason why you will do well with Finley or someone like her. You like beer rather than wine. You love football and baseball, and I'm more of a soccer guy. And so much more. Wish you well."

Levi grinned. "Thanks, man." He sobered. "I think."

"Besides, I don't like to battle for the top position. Not that I have any experience with Finley, but a guy can kinda tell."

"Ew, shit, man, TMI. But I can hear the insecurity." Levi laughed. "A man that is confident in who he is doesn't have to be on top."

"Yeah, but he wants to be."

Ryker laughed and started for the courtroom that had just opened. He walked up to a man who stood tall and spoke like someone used to commanding.

"Ready to kick some butt, Colonel?"

"More than ready, son."

Ryker entered with Levi following behind in hypervigilance mode. He'd tried to reassure Levi that there wasn't room for two bodyguards, and Levi kept saying he was wrong. Ryker had won, and when they entered the courtroom, all ready to do battle of their own variety, each had a different expectation.

Ryker was confident but not positive he would convince the judge that his client had been treated with bias and not given the benefit of the doubt, all based on old, irrelevant information. And he knew the culprit.

The colonel trusted Ryker and knew he would walk out vindicated.

Levi had wanted a partner with him because his estimation of a courtroom was television drama size. Ryker had known this one was more intimate, and he didn't worry the same. When he turned to observe Levi after they had entered, the man was more relaxed. Ryker knew he'd made the right choice.

Ryker laid out his case in smooth-flowing logic. He didn't rant or rave about what others should have seen; he pointed no fingers. He simply told the story. He had no witnesses except the Colonel, and he used him sparingly. The civilian financial business that stated he stole from them had used his military record to prove it wasn't the first time.

The company attorney tried to introduce hearsay just to get it heard, but it was stricken, and a caution was given. Ryker knew this judge could forget it. The company lawyer then tried to open a different line of attack, but the defense didn't open the door for that particular line of inquiry.

"His military record states he was asked to leave under a cloud of suspicion," stated the company attorney. He proceeded to discuss, with his client on the stand, the events he believed to be true.

Ryker cross examined. "I have previously submitted the revised paperwork to your attorney and the court, Mr. Ross. It is true that one year ago, the Colonel's record showed he was asked to retire. However, two months ago, that had been challenged, and when no evidence could be produced, they rescinded their request and offered him to return to duty. The change went into effect one week before you claimed he had taken income from your client's company. I submit that your office didn't do its due diligence in researching the information and therefore used the Colonel as a scapegoat."

"Objection. That is conjecture."

"I will show the progression that will bring the court to the same conclusion, your honor."

"Overruled. Make sure it's a clear distinction, Mr. Bennett."

"Thank you, your honor."

Ryker turned back to the business owner. "I had a forensic accountant look through the books, and they discovered the funds were taken after they left the colonel's hands. Which, I believe, was the last stop before they landed on the owner's desk and, later, his pockets. Can you verify that, Mr. Ross?"

"Objection."

"Withdrawn, your honor. Now, concerning the Winters Wear Company, who transferred their 401K deposit into their account held by your company. Your records and your bank verify the deposit amount. They agree with the account manager, and certified by Colonel, and finally, you."

"That's how the process works. Checks and balances," said Mr. Ross.

"How did you conclude that my client transferred the funds?"

"He was the last one to have access to the funds before that information was forwarded to me."

"Then help me understand. The dollar amount and the verifications are done electronically, and that information is forwarded to you, Mr. Ross, as is the policy. Correct?"

"Yes," the perspiring man answered cautiously.

"So, do I have this right? The date on the transfer into your brokerage was January 17th, and the date the deposit was verified by both the account manager and my client was January 17th, and the date and the exact amount was the same amount that you, Mr. Ross, verified was in the account on January 17th."

"Yes."

"I understand that part, but here it gets even stickier. The date that the funds were transferred to an off-shore account was in the wee hours of January 18th. Once verified, I believe only the account's manager, and the owner has access to it, and the colonel was neither. Nor was he the last one to verify the amount in the account. So, I ask how you came to the conclusion that the Colonel stole the money?"

"The military had said he was a crook. It was the natural conclusion."

"Actually, that was never formally established. And now we know that the military later rescinded their determination with their apologies and a total scrap of the issue. In fact, they asked him to return if he desired. So I ask again, how did you come to the conclusion that the Colonel stole the money on January 18th when he had no access to those funds after January 17th and before you verified the amount?"

"I don't know."

"You don't know? Might I remind you, you are under oath, sir? Might I also show you the forensic accountant report that used an IT company that traced the transfer to your office computer? Then, after some research, funds have been transferred to that same account for several years, dating back to before my client worked for you. Can you explain that, Mr. Ross?"

"I don't know."

"Well, in light of further evidence or your thought processes, this is how I perceive it to have gone. Once verified, you waited until the early hours of January 18th to transfer the money. If the client had not immediately requested their statement early, which was printed by the Colonel, you would never have been discovered because your intention was to shuffle funds, print a statement, then shuffle funds again to print another statement from another breached account. In fact, according to the accountant, you have stolen millions from your customer accounts for your own use. That isn't for me to explore, but I can guarantee someone will."

In the end, the Colonel walked out relieved and happy. Ryker was tired but satisfied, and Ryker's courtroom tango impressed Levi.

"That was actually entertaining," said Levi.

The three men walked out of the courtroom and immediately encountered an undetermined number of men pushing in on them and crowding them. Levi, who had to leave his firearms in the car, used his martial arts training and hand-to-hand skills to mow the attackers down. The colonel, who was in his fifties, did a good job of getting a few good licks in.

Ryker was being dragged, nearly unconscious, down the hall when the bailiff, the only one allowed to carry a gun in the corridor, called in reinforcements and held the attackers/attempted kidnappers at gunpoint just long enough for help to arrive. Several other bailiffs appeared with their weapons, and the party was over. The police flooded the floor immediately afterward.

Ryker's head was pounding, and his vision was blurred. It was difficult to formulate words. Damn, what did he hit his head on?

"Ryker. The police are here, and we are waiting for the ambulance. We have this covered. Just stay awake."

He couldn't nod as the blinding pain was taking most thoughts from his mind. A deep, commanding voice spoke.

"You're on duty, Captain. No sleeping on duty."

The voice was familiar, but whoever it was, it sounded like someone had peed in his cornflakes. Then the voice changed. The man was speaking to him. Calm, authoritative, sincere.

"This is the Colonel, Ryker. You have been hit by an object as yet undetermined. The ambulance is here and coming down the hallway. It's going to get a little crazy again, but you don't have to resist this time. These are the good guys. Just relax and let them do their job. We have called your Oakley and Jacquard Reynaud. Things are all good, son."

Son. The Colonel.

"Sir, can you give us some space?" asked the paramedic.

Ryker's first instinct was to fight them, but the Colonel, the man he had just defended, had told him what was going to happen. Oakley knew, and she would be sick with fear for him and you. Damn. Jac knew, and he would kick some butts and raise the protection level for all the women. Oh, his head hurt so fucking bad.

OAKLEY'S HEART WOULDN'T quit pounding. She was fired up and ready to do battle. Audra had gone too far. She'd tried to take the one thing that Oakley loved most in the world, and that would not fly. Audra had done her best to ruin Oakley and to devastate her. Now it was time to end this sick game.

"Jac, I want to go see him."

Jac and Carter spoke in unison. "No fucking way."

Oakley was feeling her strength of mind and soul come back online. Anger tended to do that to a person, and it wasn't just righteous indignation; it was undiluted fury. Her body strength had some way to go, but she was intelligent, and she wanted to expose these lunatics for who they were.

She'd heard the story of events from Jac as told by Levi, who was also staying overnight in the hospital. Evidently, Ryker's bell had been rung pretty hard, and he was getting medication to slow his functions down to help his head feel better without extra drugs and heal a little faster. She didn't care. All she knew was some of Audra's men had gotten to him at the courthouse, and they hurt him. He needed her.

This group of lunatics ruined lives, took lives, and became like gods deciding who would live and die by convincing people they didn't need the one thing that kept them successful, happy, and fulfilled. Some people didn't need medication, but for those who did, it was mandatory they be confident that it was a good thing to take.

Jac asked her, "What would Ryker say if he knew you came out of full protection to see him in the hospital? It is very possibly a trap, Oakley."

"He will be furious, but if you won't take me, I'll call an Uber."

Monroe stepped into the discussion. "Oakley, you are never to use an Uber. We can discuss the whys another time, but the answer to an Uber is always going to be no."

"You can't keep me here. I'm going to Ryker." Tears filled her eyes. "He came to me and gave me what I needed, when I needed it, and I won't do any less for him." She turned to Garrett. "Don't you understand? I have to see him with my own eyes. I need to touch him. Hold him. Be with him."

The room was full of dominant, bossy women protecting men, likely battling within themselves. She could almost hear them murmuring. Good.

"Ryker will kill us all," said Monroe.

"Likely," said Garrett.

Jac laughed mirthlessly. "Oh, no. That's a damn certainty."

"I'll get my coat," said Oakley, confident she had gotten through to these men who loved their women so completely. "I'll tell Ryker I didn't give you a choice. I was going to take an Uber."

"You need a spanking," said Jac.

"I do not. I need Ryker."

Monroe laughed. "Maybe he'll think you need a spanking, too."

Oakley rolled her eyes as the men grabbed their jackets and grumbled. Monroe looked sternly at Oakley. "We do it the right way and no other. Get me?"

"Yes."

She felt like she should attach sir at the end, but chalked it up to nerves. She wanted to go, but she was afraid to leave the protection of this overly secure house. But this was Ryker, and he needed to know she would risk anything for him. She'd risk everything.

Oakley had only spent a small amount of time with the women his friends loved, and she wanted to get in more. Bella, whom she had expected to see, hadn't come by at all, and she wondered why. Ryker said she had disappeared when Oakley had, and the coincidence of that didn't escape her. Bella was either in trouble or the trouble. It hurt her, but she knew whatever was going on with Bella would have to wait. Maybe she should call her and see if she would answer. If she was hiding from trouble, Oakley needed to let her know what kind was out here.

Hopefully, Bella would do what she suggested for once. Suddenly, a loud, angry voice exploded in her head. It was a blaring, distorted sound, but one she knew deep in her soul that she had heard before. She shivered and bent over with her hands on her ears.

"That's it. We're video calling Ryker when he can receive the call, but you aren't well, and we're keeping you here." Monroe was as adamant as she had ever heard him.

"No. Please, let me go to him. I promise. I pinkie promise I won't leave your presence. Please? I'm okay. Really."

The unexpected flashback had faded almost as quickly as it had appeared. Oakley knew that may not always happen, but she was thankful for it this time. She hoped with all she was that Ryker wanted her there and he wouldn't end what they had because of the danger she brought with her. Since the moment he laid eyes on her, she had been embroiled in some kind of trouble. He should run as far and as fast as he could, she thought. And in the next breath, prayed he wouldn't.

Garrett spoke into the room. "Take your coat off, Oakley. They are not allowing visitors today. They hope to remove that restriction around lunch tomorrow."

Oakley visibly deflated. "Oh." Then she brightened. "That's fine. I'll just sit in the waiting room."

"The answer is no," said Jac. He held up his hand when Oakley opened her mouth. "That discussion is over. We will go when they allow visitors. Protecting you in a hospital room is challenging enough without adding a shit ton of people and activities to the mix. No."

The tears raced down her cheek, unchecked. Mallory, who had come with Monroe this morning to help keep Oakley's mind off Ryker being gone for a day, gathered the other woman in her arms.

"Keep your coat on. I'll get mine. We are going for a walk."

Monroe, who knew his Mallory, said, "Mal, if you leave these grounds, we will still be talking about this next month."

Mallory rolled her eyes. "Understood... meanie."

Monroe shook his head, but smiled. "Go for a walk. It's getting cold out there, so don't stay gone for too long."

They released Levi from the hospital the next morning, and Ryker was allowed visitors at noon. The moment they got word that he could receive visitors, Oakley was dressed and waiting for her ride.

"Young lady, you remember what I said about doing as you are told the minute you are told? I'm not playing around with your safety."

"I understand, Jac. Can we go now?"

Monroe rounded the corner with his coffee in a to-go cup. "I'm not going to start off the day with hospital coffee."

Oakley could tell neither man was happy about her demanding this happen, but they didn't say anything else. She was relieved because her stamina wasn't what it was before the kidnapping. She still tired easier and had residual flashes of her psychedelic ride, compliments of Audra.

Oakley had been able to get a message to Charles that she was taking some time off. She also warned him to be careful around his sister and to keep his medications hidden. Audra was having some mental health issues herself. Oakley didn't feel bad about warning Charles. She felt it came under her duty to protect.

The ride to the hospital was quiet, as everyone was caught up in their thoughts. Oakley was full of what-ifs, and she knew that was not a good road to go down. She resolutely changed her thoughts the best she could and concentrated on getting Ryker back home. Soon they were pulling up in front of the hospital, and true to her word, she made no move to exit the vehicle until Jac and Monroe flanked her while escorting her inside the building. Jac nodded his approval.

The men were hyper-vigilant, and while Oakley appreciated it, she also realized the danger she was really in. She wondered if Ryker was in danger just by being in the hospital. She worried that this attack indicated that Ryker was now on their radar and was in an equal amount of danger as she was, maybe even more now.

"Jac, maybe I shouldn't go in," she asked outside the door of Ryker's hospital room.

"Oh, you have no choice now," said Jac with some satisfaction. "You insisted on being here, and I understand. If I don't make you work through this fear, it will stay with you. Yet it's our job to take care of you, and I get it, but it also was the dilemma. You pushed to have this happen, so you need it, and it is happening. Ryker will do better knowing you are safely under lock and key with big brawny bodyguards around you, so expect him to send you home." He smiled. "I also expect you to push back and stay."

Oakley rolled her eyes as she pushed open the door. While these men hated not getting their way, it was amazing how insightful they were. Scary, in fact. She put on a big smile as she crossed the threshold. That expression froze in place as she saw her man's face. He was swollen, scraped up, and they had wrapped his shoulder and arm to his torso. His eyes were closed, and she gave herself a quick pep talk. He's okay. He just needs some time to heal.

An arm slipped around her shoulders, giving her a side hug. Monroe was always the first to share an emotion. He would have been a great therapist. He was going to be a great dad when Mallory's baby got here. Jac spoke into the room.

"Ryker, man. I came all this way with a lovely lady, and all you can do is sleep? Rude."

Ryker opened his eyes in his puffy face and smiled. At least, she thought it was a smile, chased by a grimace. She immediately walked forward.

"Ryker, I'm so sorry about this. I shouldn't have brought you into this mess. Then you would be happy doing lawyer things and not laid up here in the hospital.

"Shh, shh, sweetling. I'm fine. I've been worse."

She tried to laugh. "I doubt it," she said with a confidence she didn't have. "When you go home, I'll go back to my apartment."

"No, you will not. I don't have the energy to get any firmer, but know you are not allowed to leave Jac's, and I've decided you aren't ever moving from my bed, so I guess you had better commission the rest of your things to get moved. When you're ready, you can open an office close to mine. Until then, you can wait until Jac finishes the job of taking care of Audra."

"Damn straight. We are formulating a plan as we speak. When are they releasing you?"

"Tomorrow. I've got a couple of Bravos babysitting me, and Kaden said he had some work to do, so he is on first shift. He said it would be quieter if he came here to work and let Ivy stay at your place. She's a little upset right now that they can't just stay home. She might be a handful."

"It's my fault," said Oakley.

"Nope, it's mine. I made the mandate," Jac said.

"I want to stay." Oakley sat in the chair by his bedside.

"I know, but I'm vetoing that because the guys will have their hands full if something happens while I'm in here. Having another to watch out for would be too much. Stay and visit until I fall back to sleep, and then go home with Monroe and Jac. This is one of those times, Oakley, that we discussed, when I was the deciding partner."

"I know what you're saying, but I'm staying."

"Sorry, baby, but you aren't. I won't get a moment's sleep worrying about you. If you want to make me feel better, go to Jac's place. But I love that you came. I know what it must have cost you mentally."

"I needed to see you," said Oakley with a sniff.

"I know, honey, and now that you're here, I'm glad to see and touch you. And when we are both recovered, and we are through this mess, we are going to have a discussion about following safety rules." There was the Ryker she knew. Chastising and confident, she needed this part of him as much as she needed the gentle side of him.

"We'll negotiate."

Chapter 15

They had stolen his woman again, and damn if he was going to let anyone escape this time. It was time to finish this. There had been a crowd at the front exit, so the guys had chosen a side exit closest to where they'd parked and walked right into a trap. When they had stepped out of the side door, they were hit with pepper spray, and while nuclear, biological, and chemical warfare training was something the military men were familiar with, it still shocked them at first exposure. That's all the kidnappers needed.

Callie's keen eyes scanned the perimeter, ever watchful. "No signs of movement yet." Her hand rested on the gun at her hip, ready to draw at a moment's notice. "When do we move in?" She was always eager for a fight, fueled by a restless energy that Garrett often tried to corral.

"Settle down, or you are not going in at all," said Garrett. Callie's grumble made Garrett's lip twitch.

Mark stood at the ready. His hands curled into fists, muscles tensed. He met Ryker's gaze and gave a curt nod, waiting for the order to advance.

Ryker knew these friends were deadly. They were the best at what they did, brought together now for a single purpose: to stop Audra and save Oakley. Ryker's heart ached at the thought of Oakley again trapped somewhere in that ruin of a building, at Audra's mercy. He swallowed hard against the bile rising in his throat. He would not lose the woman that meant everything to him. Earlier this year, he'd wondered if there was a perfect woman for him in the world, and now that he had found her and claimed her, he'd be damned if anyone was going to take her from him.

Ryker steadied his nerves and looked at each member of this Kick-Ass team, seeing his determination reflected in their eyes. They would succeed today—they had to. Too much depended on it.

"Thank you for risking everything for my everything."

"Man, I keep telling you we're family, and family trumps everything," Jac said.

"We move in together," Carter said, voice hard with purpose. "Watch each other's backs and stay alert. Audra won't give up Oakley without a fight."

Callie's lips curved into a humorless smile, and she drew her gun, the metal glinting cold. "Wouldn't want it any other way."

They approached the warehouse with cautious steps, weapons at the ready. Ryker scanned the crumbling brick facade for any signs of movement, but it appeared abandoned. Too abandoned. Ryker clenched his jaw as the operatives he called friends approached the abandoned warehouse, their boots crunching on the gravel. According to Sharlee's intel, this was where Audra's followers were keeping Oakley captive.

The dilapidated warehouse loomed ominously against the darkened sky, its windows long shattered and the once-sturdy brick walls crumbling in places. An icy wind howled through the broken panes, carrying the faint scent of rust, decay, and danger. As Carter led his team towards the entrance, every nerve in his body screamed that this was a trap.

"Remember," Jac whispered to his team, eyes scanning the area warily, "our priority is saving Oakley, but we can't let Audra slip away again. She's dangerous and needs to be stopped."

The team nodded solemnly, their eyes hardening with determination. "We'll get her, Ryker. Count on it," said Levi.

Beside him, Mark clenched his fists, ready for action, while Callie cracked her knuckles, her eyes filled with deadly intent.

Carter motioned for his team to fan out, surveilling the perimeter. This group worked like a well-oiled machine, and Ryker knew he didn't fit in with their world. Unfortunately, he had no choice, but he was hanging up his vest after this.

Ryker's first goal was to secure his sweetheart's safety, and the second was to put an end to this medication nightmare and stop Audra from hurting any more vulnerable people. The building looked empty, but he didn't trust it. His instincts told him this was too easy.

Ryker gritted his teeth as he peered around the corner, surveilling the dilapidated warehouse. At least thirty people milled about the large open space inside, clearly on high alert. They were heavily armed, and judging by their fanatical expressions, they would not hesitate to use deadly force.

"There are too many of them," Callie said. "We can't take them all, not without risking civilian casualties. When are the police coming?"

Ryker nodded, his jaw clenched. "Not soon enough." As much as he wanted to storm in there and rescue Oakley, Callie was right. They were outnumbered and outgunned. A direct assault would only end in loss of life.

His ear tingled as Sharlee's voice came through. "I've hacked into their security cameras. It looks like most of them are congregating on the first floor, but according to Kaden's drone, Oakley is being held on the second floor, in a small office toward the back of the building."

"Can you disable their weapons or communications?" Ryker asked.

There was a pause. "I can try to disrupt their radios to create some confusion, but I don't have access to their firearms. You'll have to neutralize those threats manually."

Ryker ran a hand over his beard, thinking fast. They needed a distraction, something to draw the followers away from Oakley so he could get her out of there.

Jac was thinking the same thing. "Tell Sharlee to set off a diversion like a bomb threat at the psychiatric hospital across town," said Jac.

"Or, better yet," said Carter, "is one at the facility Charles is about to discharge from. That should pull away some of their forces because Audra will want to protect her brother." Ryker looked at Carter. "Jac and Levi head around to the back of the building and cover the exits. Ryker and Callie, I will sneak in through a side entrance and get Oakley out."

Sharlee came across their communication devices. "How about a pseudo one that I only announce across their radios?"

"Try it, babe," said Jac.

Sharlee announced through their radios as though there was a response to a reported bomb threat at the healing center. They all knew that Audra would be frantic with concern. Her brother's needs created misinformed processing errors in Audra's head. She would not ignore her brother's additional needs.

As expected, Audra sent nearly a third of her followers in attendance to see to her brother's needs. It had to be good enough.

Mark nodded, checking the magazine on his pistol. "Be careful in there. These people are fanatics. They won't give up Oakley or their cause without a fight."

"I know." Jac tapped his earpiece, connecting to the others. "We're making our move. Be ready."

The followers' radios suddenly erupted in static.

"Let's move," Carter murmured, pushing open the warehouse door with a creak.

"Let's go get our girl," Jac said and started toward the warehouse flanking Carter, with Carter taking the lead and the rest of the team falling into step behind him.

They approached the warehouse under cover of darkness, weapons at the ready. Ryker signaled for them to fan out as they entered, covering each other as they advanced into the cavernous space. Their night vision goggles were useful, but if lights flooded the area, they were devastating, so Jac had each kit include a retractable attachment to their waist pack. They could throw them off without losing them. Later, if needed, they could put them back on.

Ryker bolted toward a side door of the warehouse behind Jac, his heart pounding. He never questioned Jac. Ryker knew his buddy wasn't keen on him going with them, but they did not know what they faced when they found Oakley. He prayed they didn't have to go back through the detox regimen again.

Jocelyn O'Connor, their company's online therapist, agreed when Mallory painted a picture of confusion and fearful responses, total chaos just as likely as complacency. The anti-medication movement's extremism had led them to this, but he was about to show them just how far he would go to save the woman he loved.

His instincts screamed trap, and a glance at Carter's tense expression confirmed he sensed it, too. Audra wouldn't leave Oakley unguarded. She knew they were coming.

Inside, shadows stretched across the cavernous space, while the distant dripping of water echoed throughout the building like a sinister metronome. They moved cautiously, weapons ready, as Ryker tried to ignore the gnawing fear in his gut. Failure wasn't an option; he couldn't lose Oakley, not when she meant so much to him.

"Keep your eyes peeled for any signs of Oakley or Audra's followers," Carter instructed his team, his voice barely audible above the eerie soundtrack of the warehouse. "And stay sharp. I have a feeling we're walking into something big."

As they crept deeper into the warehouse, the tension grew palpable, each member of the team acutely aware of the stakes at play and what their role was. If they couldn't save Oakley and bring Audra to justice, who knew what havoc she would continue to wreak?

Carter held up a hand to halt the team. He passed the pack he was carrying off to Levi. Ryker screened them all out of his focus and continued to follow Jac's lead. His mission was retrieval. His pulse raced as his mind rushed through the possibilities. Audra could have an ambush waiting inside. Bombs rigged to explode, men set in place to ambush them, or more. A dozen scenarios flickered through his thoughts, each more dangerous than the last.

But Oakley. He couldn't leave without her.

Ryker met Callie's gaze and saw his own fears reflected there. He drew a steadying breath and steeled himself for what was to come. This team had faced worse odds before, and he was counting on that luck and skill now.

"It's a trap," Mark said bluntly.

Callie's knuckles whitened around the grip of her gun. "There's no way she left this place unguarded. The place didn't clear out completely."

"I know." Ryker's jaw clenched as he considered their options. None were good. But only one led to Oakley, and Carter was an incredible on-the-ground strategist. Monroe was good at the overall plan A, B, and C, but Carter did the X, Y, Z, it's all going to hell, plan. His instincts were impeccable.

Jac spoke. "We go in deep anyway. Stay sharp and watch out for each other. We get Oakley. If we can, we will stop Audra, but she is not the priority."

Levi's eyes glinted with determination. "We knew this wouldn't be easy." He hefted the bag of explosives slung over his shoulder. "But we came prepared."

Mark's steady presence at Ryker's side bolstered his resolve. "We came in together. We come out together." His tone brooked no argument.

Kaden appeared out of what seemed like thin air. "I couldn't let you have all the fun."

Shadows flickered and danced across the walls in the dim light from the moon outside. The air was stale, thick with the scent of oil and rust.

They lined the walls and cautiously picked their way through the debris, looking for where their enemy was and where Oakley was hidden.

A flicker of motion caught their eye. Levi said, "There!"

Figures emerged from behind towering shelves and crates, armed and armored. At least a dozen. More than they had expected after so many left with the false bomb alert.

Ryker dove behind a stack of crates as a hail of bullets peppered the spot where he'd been standing. The team returned fire. The shots echoed through the warehouse like thunder.

Callie lobbed a grenade toward the attackers, the resulting blast sending debris flying. The girl enjoyed blowing things up way too much. Mark quickly picked off two gunners, their bodies crumpling to the floor.

Jac grabbed Ryker's arm, eyes wide. "Look!"

He pointed to a walkway that ran along the top of the shelves, at least thirty feet up. More gunmen were taking positions above them, raining death from an unassailable height. Fuck. For every attacker they took out, two more seemed to emerge from the shadows. Where the hell did she get so many followers?

Suddenly, men were pouring in through all the exposed doors. "Five Bravo here for support, sir. Six Charlie here for support, sir." Ryker could feel a collective sigh in the room from the Alpha group.

Carter said, "Glad for the support. Suppress, neutralize, and eliminate as needed to maintain the hill, boys."

With renewed hope, Ryker gritted his teeth against the onslaught, searching for a weakness in Audra's forces he could exploit. He was an attorney, for fuck's sake. He never thought he'd be playing war games for real stakes. There had to be a way. He wouldn't stop until he found it.

"Toughen up and get it done," he told himself.

Audra's followers had trapped them in a crossfire with no escape before Jac's men arrived. It must have been Kaden or Sharlee's SOS that went out. He loved these men. They had come in, fixed the imbalance of firepower, and were overcoming the odds.

Carter and the team hunkered down behind cover, returning fire when they could.

A cry of pain rang out as a bullet found its mark, slamming into Callie's thigh. Blood poured from the wound, soaking her pants.

Ryker's heart seized. "Callie!"

He started toward her, but she waved him off, teeth gritted against the pain as she applied a tourniquet to her leg. Garrett appeared out of nowhere and helped her get it fixed right.

"I'm all right," she insisted. "Focus on the mission!"

Ryker hesitated, torn between aiding this strong teammate and pressing on. The blood loss wasn't as bad as he feared, and Garrett covered his wife in full protection mode. He'd leave these professionals to handle things. But if he didn't find Audra, countless more lives would be at stake.

The choice was simple. Ryker turned away from Callie, swallowing back his guilt. She was strong—she would hold on until this was over. He had to believe that.

"Keep moving!" Carter shouted, firing at the gunners above. His team obeyed, but their progress slowed. The aggressors were being picked off rapidly, one by one, but Ryker feared that at this rate, none of them would make it out alive.

Unless...

Ryker's gaze landed on several large propane tanks at the end of an aisle, and an idea began to form. He spoke into their earpiece. "Carter, Jac, the propane tank."

Carter yelled into their comms, "Callie, get Callie to cover! Mark, lay down ten seconds of suppressing fire! The rest of you position for exit on my word."

They didn't question his orders, immediately moving to obey. Jac snagged Ryker and took off at a sprint, ducking behind shelves as bullets whizzed past. He slid behind the propane tanks, panting for breath, and studied their valves. If he could get them open, the resulting explosion would decimate Audra's forces and clear their path.

But it would also destroy the warehouse—and anyone still inside. Ryker gripped one valve in his hand, knowing what he had to do. For Oakley, he would make any sacrifice.

"Carter, I'm in position. On your word."

"Wait. Oakley is not on the second floor. I have positioned explosives on the second floor," said Mark. "Kaden will blow from the outside. On your mark."

"Jac. Ryker. Abort."

"Aborting," said Jac.

"Kaden in place."

Carter yelled, "Clear out! Out! Out!"

Ryker stayed in an area that he hoped wouldn't fall with the rest. He still needed Oakley.

He peered around the edge of the aisle, spotting Garrett and Mark carrying Callie toward the exit. The rest of the team members were close behind Audra's followers, and were too distracted by what they thought was an approaching propane explosion to notice their retreat.

Ryker smiled grimly, satisfied the teams would make it to safety. Now there was only one thing left to do.

He stepped out from behind the propane tanks, raised his gun and fired at the supports along the ceiling. The metal beams groaned and collapsed, bringing stacks of crates tumbling down to block the path behind him. It sealed Ryker in as the explosives detonated, protecting him, but it also protected Audra. And fuck all if he knew where his baby girl was.

Laughter echoed through the warehouse, cold and mirthless. Ryker whirled around to find Audra emerging from the shadows, a pistol dangling from her fingers.

"Clever, clever man," she purred, crimson lips twisting into a smirk. "But not clever enough."

Ryker raised and kept his gun trained on her, his heart pounding. Audra's followers were gone, buried under piles of rubble or fleeing from the coming inferno. Now it was just the two of them, alone at last.

"It's over, Audra," Ryker said. "Your plan has failed."

"Has it?" Audra tilted her head, eyes gleaming. "I still have you right where I want you. And I have your precious Oakley too."

Rage boiled up inside Ryker, nearly blinding him. He wanted nothing more than to put a bullet between Audra's eyes, but he couldn't. Not yet. There was still a chance she knew where Oakley was being held, and he had to get that information out of her before it was too late.

Ryker met Audra's gaze, icy calm settling over him. "If you touch her, I will end you."

"Big words," Audra scoffed. "But can you back them up?"

She raised her pistol, a clear challenge. His Oakley was likely already dead. His heart seized in his chest, but Ryker didn't hesitate, firing before she had the chance. The bullet struck Audra's gun, sending it clattering to the floor. She stared at her empty hands, eyes wide with shock.

Ryker kept his aim steady, waiting. The next move was hers.

Audra's shock melted into rage, her hands curling into fists. For a moment, Ryker thought she might charge at him, but she remained still. Calculating. Come on, bitch. I have nothing to lose.

"You're going to regret that," she said softly.

Ryker's grip tightened on his gun. "Where is she?"

Audra's lips curved into a smirk. "Somewhere you'll never find her. Not in time, at least."

Hope welled in his chest. Ryker fired again, the bullet whizzing past Audra's head. She flinched but didn't move, her smirk widening. His hands were shaking now, anger and fear twisting inside him like twin vipers. He couldn't lose control, not now. Not when he was so close.

"Tell me!" Ryker snapped. "Or the next bullet won't miss."

Audra stared at him, eyes gleaming with malice. "Go ahead. Kill me. You'll be doing me a favor."

Ryker hesitated, cursing under his breath. She was right—if he killed her now, he might never find Oakley, dead or alive. But if he didn't get the information soon, it could be too late to save her. If she was under the fallen debris, she had little time left. He was trapped, torn between impossible choices, with no way out.

Just then, a faint groan echoed through the warehouse. Ryker and Audra turned as one, eyes widening at the sight of a figure pulling themselves from under a pile of debris with the help of Jacquard Reynaud.

It was Oakley.

"Thought you might need my help," said Jac.

She was battered and bruised, her clothes torn, but she was alive. Ryker's heart nearly burst from his chest as Oakley looked up, meeting his gaze. Her lips curved into a weak smile.

"Miss me?"

Audra shrieked with rage, whirling on Ryker—but it was too late. His gun was already swinging down, striking her across the temple. She crumpled without a sound, eyes rolling back into her head.

Ryker raced to Oakley's side, pulling her into his arms. "I thought I'd lost you," he whispered, burying his face in her hair.

"You'll never get rid of me that easily," Oakley murmured. She tilted his chin up, kissing him softly.

Ryker held her close, breathing in her scent. They were together again, and this time, he wasn't letting go.

Epilogue

Sharlee stood at the front of the converted living room in her home and held up a bottle of ten-year Wild Turkey. "This, my friend," she smiled at Garrett, "will make you weep."

Garrett laughed. "Not sure Wild Turkey has the capability to do that, but I'm game."

"You'll see," she said.

She set the bottle down and gathered the bathroom-sized paper cups that had become a tradition from the first completed mission involving saving a member of their growing family.

When everyone had assembled, even Ivy looked content. No small feat after the last few days. Jac took his wife's place in front of the crowd and swept his gaze over the men and women that meant so much to him. His family. Not by biological blood but by blood, sweat, and tears. He looked at Ryker, who had Oakley in his lap. She was his all, and the relief they all had that Audra was confined to a criminal mental institution for now, awaiting possible trial, was physical.

"So, I know we all are pretty much up on what happened with Audra, but let's review so we have earned our whiskey and dinner."

Sharlee spoke up. "Right. That's my cue. Oakley helps first responders and veterans navigate their mental health once a traumatic event happens. In her first year of practice, she helped a young fireman. He had watched as a young family was burned alive in a building that was too engaged to be safe for anyone to enter. He had difficulty dealing with that reality, and Oakley was trying to help."

"That was Walt. He ultimately committed suicide," said Oakley.

"Yes, well, he had a sister. Her name is Shandra," said Sharlee. The sudden intake of breath that swept across the room told of the level of surprise at that piece of information.

"So are you saying that Shandra was holding that against me, and that's why she became my office manager so that she could what? Sabotage me? Ruin me?" Oakley was clearly becoming agitated, and Ryker murmured in her ear, rubbing her back and holding her close. It seemed to do the trick.

"Well, it becomes clearer when we add in information that was even more surprising than that." Sharlee threw Bella's picture up on the wall monitor.

Kaden took over. "We all know this is Bella, Oakley's best friend since college. She moved to Lexington with Oakley the year she opened her practice. It seems that Walter was just beginning to date Bella when he had that traumatic incident and ultimately took his life."

"What the hell?" exclaimed Jessie. Mark reached over and spoke to her ear, but her expression didn't change. In fact, as Ryker looked around the room, he saw that all the women had outraged expressions to different degrees. These women stayed by each other closer than any blood relative ever would. These women had skills of all kinds. When people talked about women having a posse, this is what they meant. He smiled because this was the type of people he wanted around his Oakley, those who would make sure to take care of business.

"But this doesn't make any sense because I would've known if she were dating someone."

"Possibly," said Kaden. "But since the time coincided with the time you were actively opening your practice, you might not have known, or she might not have told you because she wasn't sure they would last, or any number of reasons."

"Because your confidentiality is so carefully maintained," said Ryker, "it stands to reason that she wouldn't have known that her boyfriend or the guy she was dating, was seeing you professionally."

"Okay," said Oakley. "What about him telling her?"

Callie spoke up. "Again, a new relationship they were just starting; they weren't even a thing or an item yet. It really does make sense."

"And so now, what happens with those two?"

"Officer Linton has just arrested both women. Not unexpectedly, they were found together, unhappy with recent events." Jac continued. "Shandra is singing like the proverbial canary. While they weren't the masterminds in all this, they certainly did what they could to influence the outcome. For example, when Audra was upset, Shandra gave her an appointment, and they agreed on a different name so that she could go in and talk to you."

Garrett spoke. "Evidently, Shandra would not have allowed harassing calls from Audra to go through like she did, but because she wanted to torment you, she did. She was focused on making her brother's suicide your fault. And making you suffer was her end goal. Like she suffered."

"So Bella was trying to get your boyfriend from you because she lost hers, she believed, because of you?" Callie asked.

"Wait. You all saw that during one meeting?" asked Oakley.

"Listen, dinner is intense with this group," said Jac.

Levi nodded. "She was gunning for Ryker. Not sure why when she had me in the room."

A pillow thrown by someone hit him in the face. He grinned and shrugged.

"But did they do anything that was actually illegal?" asked Ivy.

Ryker answered that question. "They conspired in kidnapping and harassment, and they intended to do her harm. They could even get them for attempted murder. Those two women will not see the world outside for a very long time, if ever."

"As it should be," declared Carter.

Oakley continued the narrative. "And we know that Audra had a really tough life, and it changed her focus and her mental processes. Then, when Charles told her he was feeling so much better that he wasn't returning to the way of life they had lived before, his sister lost it. There is a lot there that I don't care to go into, ever."

"So, she focused her anger and fears on Oakley, which fell into what Bella and Shandra wanted. They helped each other," said Sharlee.

"They colluded," said Ryker.

"Hmm. So, were the incidents at the conference just that? Separate from all of this?" asked Monroe.

"Well, yes, and no. The first was Audra trying to kidnap Oakley in a place no one would likely trace to her. The second one was really a case of mistaken identity," said Ryker. "The cops called on both incidents after Linton talked to them."

"Okay, are we ready for our cup of reward?" asked Sharlee as Callie jumped up and grabbed the stack of cups to hold for Sharlee.

Becky, who had been quiet during this mission, handed them out. Mallory, the quickest to show insight into others' needs, especially the women, asked her as she sat back down, "You okay?"

"I am."

She looked over at Carter, who smiled and nodded, throwing his arm around her to pull her tight to him. He whispered in her ear.

"Hey, before we go to eat dinner, I just thought you would all like to know that Becky is pregnant."

"I wondered how long you were going to keep your news to yourself."

Becky blushed. "I didn't want to rush it. You know, in case. And I didn't want to steal Mallory's thunder."

"Girl, I have months to go, and I could use a companion."

"Good."

Jac spoke over the congratulations. "Can we carry on with this conversation at the dinner table? I'm starving."

Garrett spoke to Sharlee as they stood to go to the dining room. "This is some smooth whiskey. Good choice."

"Told you."

THE SUN HAD BARELY crept over the horizon when Ryker stood next to Oakley on their large deck outside their newly purchased home just down the road from Jac and Sharlee. The newly built, gated community was beautiful, sitting on the edge of a cliff overlooking the turbulent disaster. Ryker swore it was a man-made cliff, but Oakley said it didn't matter. He placed a protective arm around Oakley's shoulders, feeling her shiver despite the warmth of the sunrise.

"I can't believe it's over."

"Neither can I," he admitted gruffly. "But we did it together, and we survived. Now it's time for us to heal and help others do the same."

"I think I might not do private practice the way I did. How about virtual?"

"It's something to consider if you want to do that. I was thinking we could combine forces for part of the time and work on what we are passionate about."

As they stood there, embracing each other, the memories of their harrowing ordeal with Audra sometimes threatened to overwhelm them. However, they had learned that the fastest way to heal was to test your boundaries gently. Ryker was back full-time at work, but Oakley wasn't ready. Or she hadn't been before now.

They had both begun to spend more time creating their new life together rather than focusing on the horrors of the old life. The more they worked at it, the more love blossomed between them. Strength through adversity was a motto they had grabbed onto.

"Oakley, what if we used our skills to help military and first responder personnel suffering from PTSD and other trauma-related issues in a kind of community service project?" Ryker suggested. "We know first hand how hard it is to come back from a traumatic experience. Maybe we can make a difference in their lives while making one in our own."

Oakley looked up at him, her face brightening with hope. "That's a wonderful idea, Ryker. We've been through so much, yet here we are—stronger than ever. If we can bring even a fraction of that strength and healing to others, it would mean everything. It's almost worth the experience."

"Then let's do it," Ryker said resolutely, giving her a tender smile.

"But right now, I need to taste my woman."

"Again?" she laughed.

"Smart ass," he said as his hand landed on her backside. "Comply, or there is more where that came from."

"Promises, promises," she said, squealing as she ran to the bedroom.

Ryker ran his hands over her smooth skin. "This is going to be quick, but then I'll go slow. I won't last long this time." He caressed her skin, kissing her soft cheeks. He loved how needy she was. Her pussy dripped with want for him. She pushed herself into his hand; her pussy was begging for release. He moved his fingers over her swollen mound, squeezing the flesh, pulling back her cheeks so he could spear her forbidden hole with his tongue. Her cry of desperation made his cock grow even harder; it craved release from its prison and would probe for relief soon enough, but first, he wanted to taste what was in store for him next.

He stood back just far enough to run his finger over her plump, wet channel. Two fingers in each entrance penetrated her, scissoring in the back entrance, plunging into her pussy, stretching their space out as they invaded time and time again.

As he added a third finger to her ass, she screamed out at the sudden twinge of sharpness. She ground herself onto his fingers, making sure that sweet agony came through with a spicy after note. It was what she craved, and he needed to give it to her for his own satisfaction.

In the last few months, surprisingly, Oakley had found she was a bit of a masochist in her need for that bite of pain, and he the sadist for his love of giving her that twinge of pain. Sometimes it was a gentle lovemaking that enveloped the sex experience that they enjoyed, but at times like this one, when one or the other's desire raged, it was fucking.

His hand stayed on top of hers, guiding her movements, forcing her to penetrate her pussy entrance while he continued to violate her asshole. Then he shifted, pulling her hand to his cock. He kept his hand there, showing her the speed he wanted before reaching around, searching for her clit. Rolling, rubbing, then pinching hard on her clit, she became almost violent. His cock slammed into her pussy. Home at last.

RYKER STOOD BACK, HANDS on his hips, as he surveyed the freshly painted sign that hung above the entrance of their new headquarters. "Hands to Hands" it read, in bold, comforting letters. Oakley stepped up beside him, her expression reflecting the pride they both felt at seeing their dream become a reality.

"Looks great, doesn't it?" she asked, giving his hand a gentle squeeze.

"More than great," Ryker replied, squeezing her hand back and rubbing her still-flat belly. "It's the start of something incredible."

Together, they entered the building, taking in the welcoming reception area that greeted them. Soft lighting illuminated the room, casting a warm glow on the plush seating and potted plants that adorned the space. A friendly receptionist, a veteran herself, sat behind a sleek wooden desk, ready to greet any visitors who walked through the door.

"Remember," Oakley whispered, her voice filled with determination, "we're not just creating a safe space for military personnel and first responders, but also a community where they can heal and regain their strength together."

Ryker nodded solemnly, clenching his jaw as he thought about the men and women they were about to help. "Helping them by connecting them to each other. Soon, we will become redundant."

"If only," she sighed.

They continued through the building, each room meticulously designed to provide support and security for those who sought refuge there. Oakley led Ryker down a quiet hallway lined with private counseling rooms, each one soundproofed and furnished with comfortable chairs and soft rugs.

"Oakley, these are perfect," Ryker praised, feeling the tension leave his shoulders as he imagined hurting men and women finding solace within these walls.

"Thank you," she beamed, twirling a strand of her hair as she always did when she was anxious. "I wanted to ensure they felt safe enough to open up and share their experiences."

"Your attention to detail is incredible," Ryker said, his eyes filled with admiration. "I can tell you've poured your heart into this."

"Quality time, remember?" Oakley smiled warmly, her cheeks flushing slightly. "Now, let's go see the business side of the building."

The legal office and the business office flanked the community help office and gathering room. A small kitchen was on one side, and large sofas and comfy chairs created conversation areas. Books and self-help materials were strategically scattered around the large room. There was a playroom separated from the large room for those who needed the space.

At the far end of each wing was an office. There was one for Oakley and one for Ryker. He had wanted them side by side, but Oakley vetoed that. "I need my space, and being next to you will draw you into my space every free moment you have."

"I'll take it out in trade, at home." That worked.

"We designed everything here to encourage connection and healing," Oakley explained, her voice filled with passion. "And it's all thanks to our dream and our friends joining the dream, Ryker."

Ryker looked around, his chest swelling with pride and gratitude. They had created something truly special, a haven where military, vets, and first responders who put their lives on the line for others have a lifeline offered to them. Where they could find support and solace in their darkest hours. He knew that together, he and Oakley could make a real difference in the lives of those who needed it most.

"I love you, Oakley Addison. So much."

"I love you too, Ryker Bennett. So much more."

THE END

Alyssa Bailey

Alyssa Bailey is a USA Today Bestselling Author of realistic, sensual romance with a touch of suspense. A dyed-in-the-wool Texan living in the splendor of Alaska most of her life, Alyssa now divides her time between the beauty of SE Alaska and the Piney Woods of East Texas. She enjoys taking from her own experiences to create series in realistic locations to tease the reader's palate and invite them to sink into exciting adventures.

Alyssa enjoys writing consensual power exchanges between intelligent, sassy women who are not afraid to make a stand and loving men confident enough to give their woman space but masterful enough to keep her safe and content. There is *always* a "happily ever after."

Visit me online and sign up for my newsletter:
http://alyssabailey.com

Join my Facebook Group for fun and prizes:
https://www.facebook.com/groups/635273300210359/

Find me on Social Media:
https://linktr.ee/alyssabailey

Did you love *Saving Oakley*? Then you should read
Saving Sharlee by Alyssa Bailey!

HE CRAVED HER TRUST, obedience, and submission in a relationship he knew would never be equal.

Sharlee Armstrong had carefully crafted a safe existence in the shadows of life, trading information for a high price. But when she meets Jacquard Reynaud, she realizes it might be time to take a risk. He's handsome, alluring, and powerful-and Sharlee can't help but be attracted to him, but leaving the safety of her cocoon could be dangerous. Even deadly.

From his first glimpse of her, Jac knows Sharlee must be his-but he also understands getting involved with him could put her in harm's way. Hers is a world of dark exchanges and silent deals, his is a world of pretense and intrigue. Even though they resist the deep attraction they both feel, they work together to forge a working relationship, but it isn't enough. It won't ever be enough. Despite her protests, and his resistance, he finally takes her in hand for her own safety.

Her good name, livelihood, and very life are at risk if she remains with him, but despite his fears, he doesn't have it in him to let her go...for the sake of both their safety. But as they both grow closer to each other, will either of them ever truly be safe?

From his first glimpse of her, Jac knows Sharlee must be his-but he also understands getting involved with him could put her in harm's way. Hers is a world of dark exchanges and silent deals, his is a world of pretense and intrigue. Even though they resist the deep attraction they both feel, they work together to forge a working relationship, but it isn't enough. It won't ever be enough. Despite her protests, and his resistance, he finally takes her in hand for her own safety.

Her good name, livelihood, and very life are at risk if she remains with him, but despite his fears, he doesn't have it in him to let her go...for the sake of both their safety. But as they both grow closer to each other, will either of them ever truly be safe?

Read more at **http://Alyssabailey.com**

More in this *Safe and Secure* Series:
Saving Sharlee
Saving Jessie
Saving Ivy
Saving Mallory
Saving Callie
Saving Becky
Saving Oakley
Saving Finley (Fall 2023)

Don't miss out!

Visit the website below and you can sign up to receive emails whenever Alyssa Bailey publishes a new book. There's no charge and no obligation.

https://books2read.com/r/B-A-MXIL-VSXMC

BOOKS 2 READ

Connecting independent readers to independent writers.

Also by Alyssa Bailey

Safe and Secure
Saving Oakley

Watch for more at alyssabailey.com.